KALAMANCH

Anybody can be an actor

Kanan Srivastava and Neeraj Ganvir

First published in 2020 by

One Point Six Technologies Pvt. Ltd.

Wordit Content Design & Editing Services Pvt Ltd
Office No. 119-123, 1st Floor,
Building J2, B - Wing,
WadalaTruck Terminal, Wadala East, Mumbai,
Maharashtra, India, 400022.
T: +91 8080226699

ISBN - 978-93-5458-888-4

Book cover designed by:

Maria Gracia Villalba and

Sandro Arias Jauregui from Arequipa, Peru

To the actors community.

Acknowledgement

We would like to offer a warm "thank you" to our teachers at William Esper Studio: John Frey (acting), Theo Morin (movement), Nancy Mayans (voice and speech), David Kaplan(script analysis) and renowned William Esper for generously sharing their knowledge, which have been major influence in our book.

Special thanks to Roli Srivastava for ideas for creating the characters.

Lastly our deepest gratitude goes to our parents whom without nothing would be possible.

Cast Of Characters

Major Roles

Anant (Kanan Srivastava)– A shy individual with a decent demeanor, There is something about his manners that suggest his simplicity and down to earth nature. He has an unconfident look on his face.

Azim (Neeraj Ganvir)– A private man with a lean body who wears a kajol in his eyes. He is very studious in nature.

Kanika (Priya Chauhan) – A slim, smart woman with long hair and a traditional appearance. She is a passionate TV Actress who took time off from acting business to raise a family. She has a calming demeanor and a disciplined work ethic.

Kunal (Sahil Arora)– A bearded, handsome hunk, with thick black hair. He has expression which is direct to the point, and is charmingly attractive fellow.

Sunaina (Rose Sardana)– A fashion model with a confident personality and toned figure. She conveys a very presentable look.

Jheel (Siffat Gandhi) – A fashionable youngster with keen eye. Her curly hair gives a happy go lucky persona.

Ragini (Sonal Sagore)– A tan colored strong willed girl who no one dares to challenge. She often have quizzical look on her face.

Advik (Akshay Saraswat)– A individual with a confident and pompous attitude. He dresses like a highly fashionable New York.

Hiten (Amit Poddar)- A chubby mean guy who is Salman Khan fan. He is a bully and hits on every girl from the class.

About the Author

I am Kanan Srivastava originally from New Delhi, India where I grew up and attended both high school and college. I started to act in school plays and public gatherings, however, my parents didn't think that acting was a feasible way to make a living, so I went to college for engineering and studied computer science. Even though I completed my college degree, I never stopped acting. During holiday breaks, I enrolled in workshops that helped me to get a basic knowledge about the craft of acting. Following my graduation, I moved to Mumbai. In Mumbai I auditioned for several film and television productions and was cast in several roles for web series. It was during this time I noticed limitations in my acting due to lack of formal training. One of my acting teachers recommended I read the book "The Actors Art and Craft" by William Esper. I was very inspired, and I moved to New York where I took his two-year, full time acting program. My time at The William Esper Studio made me realize good actors need a broad education. It's a great big world. Encountering other cultures will teach you to appreciate just how different and how similar we humans are. Travel. Grow up. Live life. It seems simple, but it's really important. There's no substitute for experience. That's my primary reason for wanting to expand myself, my craft and encouraging social changes in society through my work. For the same purpose I wrote "Kalamanch". The subject matter is centered on concept that anybody can be an actor regardless of their physical, mental and social circumstances.

- Kanan Srivastava

I am Neeraj Ganvir, from the Orange City Nagpur, India. Since childhood I developed an affinity towards performing arts like dance and theater. Having a knack for multitasking, I pursued a degree in computer science, and I kept honing my skills as an actor by doing acting workshops and theater plays. Honest confession! I started acting because I wanted to become famous, I was young and did not know anything about the real world of acting. But as I jumped in, I was astonished to see how much discipline, dedication, devotion, and determination is needed to become a good actor. These four D's did not scare me instead made me curious and obsessed about it. I started reading theater plays and performing in them seriously. I practiced various acting exercises mentioned in acting books. I even developed a daily routine of vocal and movement exercises and practiced all of this for years. And now when I look back and ask why did I do all of this? My answer is because I am really interested in becoming a good actor. This overcame the stupid notion of becoming famous and made me more inclined towards honing my craft as an actor. As an avid learner of the craft, I moved to the New York City where I studied the actor's art and craft at William Esper Studio. The education broadened my knowledge by giving exposure to plethora of acting techniques and related subjects. All the experience I accumulated over these years made one thing clear that an Actor needs to be always a learner. I believe it's the best gift an Actor can give to herself/himself. To promote, empower and make an impact, I decided to write the "Kalamanch".

- Neeraj Ganvir

Contents

Chapter 1

Applause filled the auditorium as the spotlight brightened a small portion of the pitch-black stage. From the darkness, the silhouette of a slim and tall woman walked towards the center of the stage, with an award in her hand.

As the bright light shined on her, one could see the happiness radiating on her face. She was smiling and tearing up with immense joy!

She composed herself, took a few deep breaths before talking.

"I'm really thankful for—"

The loud banging on the door woke a mumbling Kanika from her sleep. She got up from the couch, looked at the watch and immediately realized that she was going to be late for work. How could she have dropped off to sleep on the couch, after getting fully dressed for work? And had such a vivid dream, to boot. Shit!!

She rushed to open the door. "Coming... Coming!" she exclaimed and grabbed her belongings. Opening the door, she acknowledged her maid and said, "Come in, and bye! I'm going."

"Say I will see you soon" the maid corrected her. Oh yes, it was necessary to say, "You'll see me soon", to her maid.

"Yeah Yeah. I will see you soon! Okay?" Kanika said. She had to remind the maid to lock the door securely after she was done with her work.

"Okay!" the maid replied.

***

Salman Khan's 'Dabangg' title track was blaring from the speakers in the bedroom. On the walls were a few posters of Salman Khan, and some posters of famous female porn stars. Motivated by *Bhai's* music, Hiten was working out, pumping his biceps with a dumbbell, pretending he was Salman Khan himself. At the end of his exercise routine, Hiten swaggered to the mirror, and flexed his body, smiling with pride. He donned his flamboyant outfit and went out the door.

On his way out of the apartment, Hiten strutted down the stairs like Salman Khan. In the parking lot, the children from the apartment watched him and sniggered.

"Hey, little boy! Come here, I want to ask you something", Hiten ordered, beckoning to one of the kids. The boy sidled up to him reluctantly. "Do you hear any background music when I walk by?"

"What do you mean?" the little boy asked, confused. "Like *Hud hud hud Dabangg?*" Hiten hummed the tune. "No, *big brother, I don't know..."* replied the kid.

"Are you deaf? Tell your dad to get you a hearing aid", Hiten bullied. Before the kid could protest, Hiten grabbed the chocolate the kid held in his hand, and ordered, "Leave now. And don't look back!" He popped it into his mouth and walked away leaving the kids staring at him.

***

It was another busy day in Andheri, Mumbai. Everyone was preoccupied with their own lives — some trying to make it to their work, schools, and colleges on time, street vendors calling out their wares to attract customers, auto rickshaws looking for a fare, the honking of buses and cars crowding the road. Nothing seemed out of the ordinary.

Anant was looking for his acting studio. He stood next to the Bharat petrol pump which was crowded with motorists and car owners trying to fuel their vehicles before zooming out to their next destination. But Anant was trying to grab the attention of the pedestrians. He needed to ask for directions.

"Sir, do you know where Kalamanch is?" Anant inquired of a man walking past him in a hurry.

"No!" the pedestrian replied, barely breaking a step.

Anant sighed. He could not afford to be late on the first day of class. He picked up his phone and dialed his instructor's number for directions. She was his best bet now.

"Hello, Kanika Ma'am! I've been trying to locate the studio, but I can't find it." He got straight to the point as soon as Kanika answered his call.

"Where are you now?" she asked.

"I'm at the Bharat petrol pump", Anant exclaimed.

"Take the lane on the left side of the petrol pump, and it's the sixth building to your right, on the first floor."

Anant followed Kanika's instructions and entered the lane next to the petrol pump, but he still could not find the place.

"Ma'am! I'm unable to locate the building." He anxiously expressed. "Hold on! I'll send someone to pick you up."

Anant noticed a building with a small sign board with the words "Kalamanch Theatre Group" on it.

"It's alright Ma'am, looks like I've found the place." "That's good!" Kanika exclaimed in excitement on the other end.

Anant disconnected the call, adjusted the backpack on his shoulder, took a deep breath and entered the building.

***

Anant hastily entered the studio breathing heavily as he ran up the stairs, the class was already in session. A young girl in a pair of jeans and a red, sleeveless top was at the front of the class, introducing herself.

"I am Jheel, but friends call me Z. I am an aspiring actress", she began.

Anant looked at Jheel and was mesmerized by her. He thought she looked stunning in the red top and her self-confidence made her even more interesting to him. While staring at her in amazement, Anant dropped his pen.

Kanika noticed Anant at the door and asked him to come in. She pointed to an empty seat. Anant walked towards the seat still looking at Jheel and becoming self-conscious of it while sitting.

Once he settled down, Kanika turned to Jheel and asked, "Jheel, would you mind starting over once again?"

"Hello everyone", Jheel smiled and started again with confidence. "I am Jheel, but friends call me Z. I am an aspiring actress. I live in Bandra

West. I love listening to songs — especially by Lizzo, Billie Eilish, and Kesha. I have been acting since I was in school, and even in college. I love watching movies of Federico Fellini and I admire Meryl Streep. I hope to be like her someday... And that's about me!" she concluded in confidence.

The entire class smiled at her as Jheel walked back to her seat making an eye contact with Anant.

"That's lovely, thank you Jheel", Kanika complimented. "Anant, it's now your turn." Anant is startled at hearing his name called out by Kanika. "Can you introduce yourself and tell us something interesting about yourself?" Kanika insisted Anant on sharing about him.

Anant got up clumsily from his seat and dragged himself in an under confident manner to the front of the class. Facing a class full of people, he hesitantly started looking just towards Kanika and trying to avoid his fellow classmates.

"*Namastey!* My name is Anant, and I am 30 years old." He spoke in Hindi, his voice mechanical, like a robot. "I love making friends. I am from Shahjahanpur. We live in a joint family... I moved here after my wedding, but I live alone now. Two months ago, I was... I..." He froze and his open mouth looked like he was trying hard to gather his thoughts. He tried to overcome the anxiety but was failing at it.

"It's okay Anant. You can tell us the rest when you are comfortable", Kanika intervened and unburdened him off the pressure.

Anant smiled at her nervously and returned to his seat next to Jheel. She threw him a sympathetic glance.

"Sunaina?" Kanika said, turning towards another girl in the class. She was tall, had a toned figure, and wore makeup that suited her face.

Sunaina walked confidently to the centerstage with an erect posture and her head held high.

"Hi! My name is Sunaina and I am a fashion model. I love adventure sports like ziplining, paragliding, and so on. A little fun fact about me is I love hula-hooping." Sunaina was proud of herself and delivered her introduction flawlessly.

"That's very good, Sunaina", Kanika complimented her, impressed. "Hiten?"

On hearing his name, Hiten threw a look like Salman Bhai. All looked at him and his flamboyant clothes that were not at all fitting. He walked to the front of the class imitating Salman *Bhai*. Despite his workout routine, he was a slightly chubby man in his mid-thirties and wore fashionable clothes that did nothing to improve his appearance. He completed the look with black sunglasses and Salman Khan's signature blue bracelet.

"Hello everyone! My name is Hiten. I am a fan of Salman, who's a superman to me. My favorite movie is Dabanng, and there is no one bigger than *Bhai.* I can do anything to become an actor.' Hiten waited expectantly, his attitude cocky.

"Oh really? So, what do you mean by you can do anything?" Kanika shot him a question.

"Anything as in..." Hiten lowered his hands to the end of his shirt and with swift movement pulled up his shirt and took it off like Salman Bhai. All were astonished and laughed at his stupidity. Hiten was stinking really bad because of his sweaty oiled body. All were disgusted by it. Jheel covered her nose, Sunaina started flapping her hand in front her nose.

Kanika herself was surprised. "Please stop, Hiten! This is not required to become an actor. Thank you for the show. Now, go back to your seat", Kanika exclaimed, deadpan.

"My pleasure!" Hiten winked at Kanika, as he walked back to his seat wearing his shirt. "Azim?" Kanika called out.

Azim was clearly disgusted by Hiten's distasteful exposure but composed himself and walked to the centerstage, his demeanor calm.

"Hey! My name is Azim; I run a coffee shop. I am so into films, and I love independent and offbeat cinema. My favorite actor is Manoj Bajpayee, and my favorite movie is Aligarh. I wish to be a trained and seasoned artist like Manoj

Bajpayee someday."

"Very good, Azim." Kanika smiled. "Thank you! Now, Ragini?"

Ragini sitting in anticipation of her name being called out. She looked at Kanika and expressed a sigh that it's finally her chance. Ragini was dusky, with a bold personality. She strode to the front of the class. "Hi, my name is Ragini. I don't usually like being called in last; I hope this is the only time." She glared at Kanika imposing her point of view before continuing. "Anyways...in short, I am Ragini, and I am here to learn acting. That's it!"

Before Kanika could respond, Ragini walked back to her seat.

"That's good, Ragini." Kanika was taken aback by the straightforward attitude however she accepted it and looked at the rest of the class. "Well! I think it's my turn now." Before she could start, she was interrupted by a late entrant.

"Hi... May I?" A young man cut in. He was well-built and looked like a male model. "Hello there! Come in. Advik, right?" Kanika asked him.

"Yes", he said confidently.

"You are late...which is not acceptable in my class", she declared and made her point. She turned to the rest of the class. "Is that clear, everyone?"

"Well, I was feeding my dogs", Advik reasoned while taking his seat. Sunaina and Jheel exclaimed in awe.

"Okay, then. Come, introduce yourself." Kanika pointed towards the stage. Advik changed his direction and got to the centerstage with full confidence and charisma.

"Well...I am Advik, and just like the meaning of my name, I am *unique*. You may have seen me before since I work as a model and have done ads for quite a few top brands. I like playing golf, polo, and horse-riding. My favorite Actor is Uday Cho.. Chhabra..", Advik smiles sarcastically. "And my favorite actress is you." Pointing finger at Kanika and smiled. "I am the son of a business tycoon..."

"Wait!" Kanika interrupted him. "I just want to know who you are, not your family background."

"Umm...okay. Well, I would like to be an actor because I have the looks and the charisma. If a cartoon like Manvir Singh can become someone, then why can't I?"

Kanika was surprised at Advik's statement. "That is nice, but you know what...you just know his success story, not the dedication, devotion, and determination that he put into his craft to achieve what he has today. I truly respect him, and you should too." She gestured to Advik to take a seat. Finally, she got to the task of introducing herself.

"Hello everyone! My name is Kanika Arora and I... uh...live in Versova, Andheri. You might recognize me from my previous work in TV.", Jheel, Sunaina and Azim approved her by a nod. "I was on a break from acting, and that's a story for another time. So here I am, the director of the Kalamanch theater group. I have always wanted to teach creative drama and thank goodness, I am finally able to do it! You are my first creative drama class and I thank you for choosing me as your instructor." Kanika smiled as the entire class acknowledged her words. "I hope that these classes are going to be interactive and each one of you is going to participate actively." Everyone nodded.

"So, my first question to you is...what is acting?

While everyone contemplated on the question, Jheel raised her hand in excitement. Kanika called on her.

"Ma'am, I believe acting is reacting. It's basically living the life of different characters." "Good! That's a nice attempt but I am looking for a specific answer. Anyone else?" Kanika encouraged everyone and pointed at Anant.

Anant was startled again at hearing his name. "Ahh...umm...Ma'am, I don't know what acting is", Anant stammered. "Nothing to worry about. Just say whatever comes to your mind."

"Ma'am, acting is a debate…. Ahhh… mmm.. a.. controversy — something that can strike the hearts of the ones who watch it." Anant tried to rephrase what Jheel said. But was clearly unsuccessful and was nowhere close to it.

Everyone giggled. Kanika was also in amazement of what he is talking about and exclaimed. " Okay Anant. Nice try".

"Acting is entertainment, Ma'am. It is what Salman *Bhai* does. Bang Bang!" Hiten exclaimed excitedly, pretending to shoot bullets out of his fingers.

"It's just memorizing lines and delivering them", Advik intervened while Hiten was shooting bullets.

"What you said is a small tip of the iceberg. Actually, acting as a whole is - HUGE..." Kanika responded and emphasized with her hands. "Anyone else.?" Kanika waited patiently.

"Acting is an activity in which the story is told by means of its enactment by an actor who adopts a character, who lives truthfully in the circumstances of the play, immerses himself in the world of play and the character he/she is playing. By continuous use of acting tools and techniques", Azim gave his definition of acting.

Hiten smacked Azim on his head, taunting and teasing him.

"That is a great answer, Azim." Kanika complimented in an overwhelming tone. "But can anyone give me the definition in one single line?"

As if in answer, a man appeared at the classroom door. He was dressed in business casuals, was handsome, had a lean, athletic body with a beard that cupped his face perfectly. His confidence made all the heads in the class turn in his direction. Sunaina was awestruck and started checking out him from top to bottom.

"Acting is living truthfully under imaginary circumstances", the man asserted. His voice matched his looks and he continued. "Am I right? Or

Am I right?" the man exclaimed.

"Shit! You stole my answer", Sunaina blurted, her eyes pinned on the man. He laughed and marched into the class with his charm.

"Everyone...this is my partner in crime..", Kanika introduced the man proudly.

"I am Kunal, Kanika's husband. I am here to help with her very first acting class." Kunal smirked.

Shit! Sunaina sighed in disappointment upon learning that Kunal was taken and no longer available for her.

"And you are also late! This is not allowed in my class, okay?" Kanika playfully chided her husband. Advik was quizzically looking at Kanika.

"Okay." Kunal held his ears with his hands as a sign of apology.

"So..." Kanika turned to the class. "Acting is all about how you express yourself truthfully in an imaginary world."

Everyone pondered over what Kanika said. Kanika welcomed their curiosity and briefly explained how *an actor was just an instrument.*

She used illustrations and explained how to turn your body into a single instrument, connecting various elements such as voice, body, and inner emotions. She also explained the concept of *contact, behavior, and motion* for the basic understanding of the human body. Looking at their puzzled faces Kanika calmed them. "We will learn about these things in much more detail...so let's start." Thus began their new acting course.

Chapter 2

Blackout. Only the silhouettes of the participants were seen standing in the studio.

"Lie down on the floor", she instructed.

All obeyed her promptly and lied down on the floor in a circle.

"Now let us test your listening skills. One of you start counting from one and another should follow with the next number. No two people can call out at the same time. Let's get started", Kanika clarified and explained the rules.

"One..." Sunaina started the count. "Two." Kunal joined in.

"Three!" Jheel and Anant screamed in unison.

"Stop. Start once again", Kanika instructed, turning on the light. "It's a listening exercise. Hear each other. Wait, analyze, and then speak."

She turned off the light so that the exercise could begin again. "One", Anant began this time.

There was a brief pause since each person listened and waited for the other to jump in. "Two..." Kanika added to the count.

"Teen", Hiten had to be different and announce it in Hindi.

"Char! Sorry...four", Azim corrected himself as he went on with Hitens's Hindi version. All giggled and went back to counting. "Five", Jheel announced cautiously.

"Six." Sunaina quickly announced after Jheel.

"Seven", Kanika took a while listening and then added, taking part in the activity once again. "Eight", Kunal quickly announced.

Sunaina and Anant uttered the number *nine* at the same time impatiently. "Shit!" Anant exclaimed disappointedly, followed closely by Sunaina's "Sorry."

"Oh God!" Jheel sighed. Everyone took a deep breath, knowing that they would have to repeat the exercise.

"Start over", Kanika instructed. She turned to Advik. "Why aren't you participating, Advik?"

"I didn't like the exercise", Advik responded indifferently.

"C'mon, guys! We have to do this every day", Kanika reminded the class. "That means you too, Advik", she added.

"This is lame", Advik grumbled, but Kanika ignored him. She switched on the light and asked the participants to sit up.

"Do you know how important it is to listen?" she asked.

"Madam, we just have to recite the dialogues and nothing else, then what is the necessity of all this bullshit?" Hiten quizzed.

"Mind your Language Hiten", Kanika warned.

"No, listening allows you to live in the moment", Azim answered confidently.

"Yeah sure, you should know!" Hiten mocked Azim.

"What Azim said is right. Listening connects you to your partner so that you can react to them well. Then it all looks natural. Also, it saves us from the overlapping of lines and talking over each other", Kanika explained.

The class nodded. Some of them even took notes.

"Now, let's all take a break and I want you to utilize this time in getting to know about each other", she said, dismissing the class.

***

During the break time, Jheel, Sunaina and Ragini were in the bathroom. Jheel was in a bathroom stall and Sunaina was touching up her make up in front of the mirror while Ragini leaned against the sink and watched Sunaina.

"Do you want to put some on?" Sunaina asked Ragini. "No, I'm good. I don't use make up *at all!*"

Jheel came out of the stall. Ragini moved away from the sink and made way for Jheel. "No makeup? So, you like it all natural?" Sunaina asked.

"Wow! That's a nice shade", Jheel intervened and complimented, eyeing the product Sunaina was using. "Can I try it on me?" Jheel asked.

Sunaina gave it to Jheel, and watched her apply it on her face.

"Wow! It looks good on you", Sunaina complimented. "You're going to floor everyone." Jheel blushed, but also managed to look smug at the same time.

"Enough already." Ragini looked bored. "You girls are always trying to get attention from the boys."

"Cheer up. You know... I had my eyes on Kunal. But sadly, he's taken." Sunaina pouted.

"He looks old", Jheel remarked.

"So what? I don't care", Sunaina boasted.

"I hate boys." Ragini added to the conversation.

"Yeah, me too", Sunaina sarcastically added. "That's why I like men, not boys."

"Then we only have Kunal, Advik, Anant, and Azim..." Jheel laid out the names, pausing for a moment before gathering her thoughts. "Well, I think Azim is just a studious boy, Kunal is a bit old and Hiten is just an Asshole!"

"You are a keen observer, huh?" Sunaina commented.

"Alright! Let's go now", Ragini led the girls out of the restroom. She couldn't take any more of it.

***

Azim, Anant, and Hiten were chatting in the classroom during the break. Advik did not want to take part in the small talk and pretended to be busy.

"So, where are you guys from?" Azim inquired.

"I am from Shahjahanpur", Anant replied. "But I've been trapped here… I mean living in Mumbai for quite a while now."

"I am from Mumbai as well. I have a coffee shop", Azim told them.

"Great! I am bringing my next girl to your coffee shop. Free coffee!" Hiten enlightened.

"Sure..." Azim responded hesitantly. "What about you?" he asked Advik, turning towards him.

"Mumbai, Bro!" "I live in Bandra." Advik answered boastingly. "Nice!" Azim aknowledged. Jheel entered the class with Ragini walking behind her.

Hiten whistled at Jheel and started to sing and dance to Salman Bhai's song *"Mashallah... Mashallah!"* staring at her. Jheel gave him a dirty look.

"Eh Loser*!* What's it with you? Just get out of here", Ragini remarked condescendingly.

"Oh, you! I didn't even see you in this dark." Hiten mocked her complexion, hoping to shut her up.

"Let me give you a tight slap and then you'll probably see", Ragini retorted. "At least this way, you'll get to touch me." Hiten winked at Ragini.

She stomped to the corner where Jheel was on her phone.

"Bro, control yourself. I think it's a little too much." Anant tried to stop Hiten. Hiten was getting out of line, insulting people based on their appearances.

"It's nothing, bro! At least I am giving her some attention." Hiten shrugged it off.

"I'll be back in two", Azim excused himself to get away from Hiten's company and excused himself. Anant followed him out. It was obvious that they felt uncomfortable with what had just happened and didn't want to be near Hiten.

Ragini carried her anger to Kunal who had just entered the class. "Sir, please tell Hiten not to bother me. He is a pervert", she accused and complained about him.

"Just call me Kunal", Kunal corrected her. "And don't mind Hiten. He's just joking around. Take it easy."

Aghast that Kunal brushed off her concerns, Ragini stormed out of the class.

***

After the break, the class reconvened and, Kanika had Hiten and Ragini facing each other. Kanika was starting the repetition exercise.

"I like your figure", Hiten commented.

"You like my figure?" Ragini asked, totally astonished. "Yes, I like your figure", Hiten repeated.

"What do you mean you like my figure?"

"You know, it's great! Just amazing!" he expressed voraciously, and outlined her shape with his hands.

"Jerk! I will give you a tight slap.."

"Yeah sure... go ahead touch me darling." Hiten tried to provoke her.

"You asshole! Fuck you", Ragini yelled. "Yeah! Fuck me! C'mon!" Hiten taunted, not ready to back down. "C'mon, lay a finger on me and feel me. It'll be fun."

"You fucker! I'm going to kill you!" Ragini threatened.

"Yeah I am fucker. Kill me while you Fuck me!!", Hiten shouted.

"You Bastard!! You got a small dick that doesn't even get hard!", Ragini thrashed Hiten.

"Come here and I will show you.", Hiten provokes Ragini opening his zip.

Kanika intervened, stopping the two before the situation gets out of hands. "Stop! Stop! You aren't supposed to get physical in this exercise. You must stay at least six feet apart. Understand!" Kanika stated authoritatively.

Ragini stepped back. "Okay, But he provoked me", she mentioned.

"I know. But this is the exercise, and most people find it hard to understand", Kanika explained, trying to calm her down.

"This exercise is a lot of fun. We should do it every day", Hiten suggested, delighted that the exercise gave him permission to express his fantasies openly and to annoy his classmates, especially Ragini.

"Yes, we will be doing this exercise daily. This is to develop your spontaneity as well as the authenticity to the role you are playing. It makes you drop your guard and builds your impulses", Kanika reminded.

"Sunaina and Anant, you are next."

***

The Next day, Advik entered the classroom sneakily so that Kanika wouldn't notice him. "Advik, you are late once again. Why?" Kanika catches Advik without looking at him.

Advik gives up and stands upright from his ducking stance, "Well, on my way to the class in my Audi, I noticed an old lady waving for a lift. Being the generous person that I am, I couldn't stop myself from helping her out. So, I dropped her home", Advik responded.

Advik's so-called act of kindness impressed Jheel and Sunaina and they were awed, but Kanika saw right through his excuse.

"Oh, is that it? Can you stop giving me fake excuses and just be punctual?" Kanika asked. Advik stared at her mumbling.

"Do you understand?" she asserted further.

"I wasn't lying at all. Advik Singh never lies. I told you exactly what I did. There was nothing fake about it", Advik asserted.

"Alright, go take your seat now", Kanika instructed. "Now, who's next? Jheel? Come on."

Anant heaved a sigh of relief. Kanika forgot that it was his turn with Sunaina before Advik interrupted the class.

"I didn't get a chance to rehearse", Jheel conveyed. "Why?" Kanika questioned.

"Because Advik was not available", Jheel replied. "And why is that, Advik?" Kanika questioned Advik.

"Well, I was at the hospital donating blood. I didn't find time for the rehearsals", Advik gave an excuse and looked angrily at Jheel for snitching on him.

"Oh really? This is not good at all, Advik. Excuses for everything! You need to rehearse with your partner." Kanika chided, her voice furious. "I want you to see me in my office now."

***

Advik followed Kanika to her office.

Kanika gestured to the chair across from her desk on which Advik sat down. "Advik, I already warned you about coming late, but you have not taken it seriously." Kanika grilled Advik.

"I think my reasons were genuine. Honestly Ma'am, in Mumbai's traffic, you end up being either early or late. And fifteen minutes is like nothing", Advik tried to reason with her.

"I don't think so", Kanika retorted. "You cannot be thirty minutes late for the class and you've showed up late to class every single day."

"Well Kanika…. Ma'am... sometimes, I get late because I do a lot of modelling work for big brands." Advik bragged about his work.

"Then you shouldn't be wasting your time here. Go do your modelling assignments, Advik. This class needs commitment. I am sorry I have no place for you. Not anymore!" Kanika chided.

"What?" Advik asked in surprise. "I am your Star student. Even Kunal come late. You don't say anything to him." Advik questioned and blamed Kanika for being biased. Enraged at hearing Advik questioning her, Kanika thrashed at him.

"You are no longer my student, let alone my star student. Here's your refund." Kanika returned Advik's money to him. He grabbed it from her and tore it apart in front of her. He stormed out the of the cabin slamming the door on his way out.

Meanwhile in the men's bathroom, Azim washed his face and meticulously applied moisturizer to his face. He heard when someone flushed the toilet in the stall behind him. The stall door opened and Hiten walked out, zipping up his fly.

"Hey, smarty pants, what are you applying to your face? Give me some", Hiten said mockingly. "It's just moisturizer", Azim replied.

"So what? Give me some", Hiten ordered.

"Sure, but first wash your hands", Azim insisted.

"Fucker, just give it", Hiten demanded, and he grabbed the tube out of Azim's hands and began applying it to his face.

"I didn't say you could borrow it", Azim snapped back at him.

"Yeah, so what? What are you going to do about it?" Hiten remarked and stepped menacingly towards Azim.

Azim took a step back. "Okay, I'm sorry", Azim pleaded.

"Remember to stay in your place around me. Understand?" Hiten threatened. "Hmm…" Azim muttered.

"What are you murmuring? Say it properly. Do you understand?" Hiten asked. "Yes, I understand", Azim replied.

Hiten tries to hand Azim his moisturizer. "It's okay. You can keep it", Azim squeamishly denied the moisturizer as Hiten held it with his unwashed hands, and opened the door to leave the men's room. He was pushed aside by Advik who stormed in furiously and punched the door of one of the stalls.

"What happened to you?" Hiten asked.

"Nothing. She's just an over-smart bitch. I'm done with her and these stupid classes",

Advik responded. "Who?" Hiten asked.

"Your Kanika ma'am. After doing TV shit shows she thinks too much of herself", Advik tarnished Kanika. He stomped out of the restroom.

"So, you're leaving?" Hiten asked. "Oh, he already left."

***

Anant and Sunaina were the only ones left in the classroom during the break. Sunaina was hunched in one corner of the room, listening to a voice message on her cell phone. Anant was drinking water, watching her discreetly. Their eyes met. She gave him an absent-minded smile.

"How long did they say the break was?" Anant asked.

Sunaina, still listening to the message, used her finger to gesture that she was busy and mouthed the words, "Sorry." Once done, she asked, "Sorry, what did you say?"

"I asked how long..." Anant spoke loudly.

There was a short pause as Anant realized just how loud he was and tried to gather his thoughts and get his tone in check.

"How long was the break supposed to be?" Anant asked again in his normal tone.

"I think around ten minutes", Sunaina answered, continuing to check the messages on her phone. When she looked up again, Anant was trying to say something to her, and his lips were moving.

Sighing, Sunaina took her earphones out. "What?" she asked.

Embarrassed, Anant took a few steps back to compose himself. There was a long awkward pause while Sunaina waited for Anant to repeat what he had just said.

"I was saying that you have really beautiful eyes." Anant finally managed to say the entire sentence without stuttering.

"Oh, wow, I am..." Sunaina blushed at his compliment.

"Sorry, I wasn't trying to hit on you. I'm just complimenting you", Anant explained himself. He looked uncomfortable, wondering if he had crossed a line.

"I didn't take it that way but thank you." Sunaina smiled.

"But still, I didn't have any ulterior motive for saying that", Anant added to make sure that Sunaina didn't misunderstand his intention.

"No, it's okay. I get that it was a compliment", Sunaina assured. "So, you're from around here?" Anant asked.

"Oh no, I'm from Delhi. I moved here around six months ago", she answered. "So, you live nearby?"

Sunaina nodded. "Do you live around here?" she asked. "I live in Goregaon", Anant replied.

"Oh! It's a good place."

"I live alone. My wife and I got divorced some time ago. It's just been a few months, to be honest", Anant opened up hesitantly. This takes him back to the time he fought his mother who loved him the most. Still he fought with her to go to Mumbai after Sonali.

A terrace with an iron bed, on which pickles were drying. Anant's mother was drying up clothes on the wire as Anant approached her to convince her to let him go to Mumbai. Anant mentioned about his love interest Sonali to his mother. Anant's mother got upset and raised her voice, "That girl messed up your head! You were such a good lad and now you have become headstrong and want to go to Mumbai city of thugs".

Anant tried to assure his mom, "Sonali loves me very much". Anant's mother snapped at him, "I will give you a tight slap! You are a fool. You didn't study anything, you are not smart so she is taking advantage of you. She will take all your money and run away. She was the mistress of the mayor of neighboring village. She is infamous among people for this kind of behavior. She is a wicked woman."

Anant neglects it and is adamant in his decision to go to Mumbai even after his mother's lashings! Anant snaps back saying, "I will go to Mumbai anyway! I will do my own thing! I will never leave her because I love her. I don't care what people talk about her." Anant storms out.

Sunaina snapped her fingers in front of him to bring him back to the present.

Meanwhile Kanika entered the classroom and clapped her hands to draw the students back. "Advik won't be a part of this group anymore because according to him, he's already a star."

With this bald statement, she walked back to the office, leaving them all curious about Advik's sudden dismissal.

Kunal followed Kanika into her in a hurry and seemed impatient. As he entered the cabin, Kunal hesitantly asked, "Did she call you?" Kunal asked.

"Who?", Kanika questioned.

Kunal hesitantly said, "Jiya?". With frustration Kanika replied rolling her eyes.

"Yeah. We just..." Kanika busied herself with some papers on her desk. After a few moments, Kunal asked, "What did you talk to her?" "Nothing. It was just a casual conversation", Kanika replied.

"Don't trust her words." Kunal coached her.

"Yes, I know", she reassured Kunal. "I trust you."

"You know I love you." Kunal moved closer to her and maneuvered the situation. Before they knew it, their hands were all over each other, and he had unbuttoned her blouse. She pulled his shirt from where it was neatly tucked into his trousers. There was a loud knock on the door, and it opened before they could straighten up.

"Ma'am, there are some questions that I..." Hiten's voice trailed off noticing their state of disarray. Kanika tried to gather her air of authority around her. For once, Hiten was at a loss for words looking at Kanika's cleavage revealed by an unbuttoned blouse and he stammered, "It's nothing... I forgot to... I'll ask you tomorrow if I remember it", he was turned on but he gathered himself and left hurriedly. Realizing that her blouse revealed a lot more to the pervert like Hiten, Kanika adjusted her blouse hastily and threw a look at Kunal.

Chapter 3

Later that evening, Kanika in her dining room danced to *Aaj phir jeene ki tamanna hain,* a 70's Bollywood song, with a glass of wine in her hand. Swaying to the music, she was setting the table for candle light dinner. She heard a knock on the door. Expecting Kunal to join her, she sprayed the room with a lavender air freshener and rushed towards the door excitedly. As she opened the door she was surprised to have found Jiya, the same person Kunal and Kanika were discussing about in the Kalamanch studio office. .

"You?" Kanika tried to shut the door, but Jiya placed her foot on the threshold. "I thought I should talk with you once, face-to-face", Jiya replied.

"Listen, I don't want to talk to you", Kanika bashed at her, wishing she could smash the door on Jiya's face.

"We were friends before. Won't you invite me in!" Jiya reminded and insisted.

"Okay, come in", Kanika pitied on her. "But I am in a good mood, so please don't ruin it. Whatever it is, tell me quickly. What do you want?" Kanika demanded.

"I want to confess something to you….", Jiya informed. "Kunal and I slept together…last Saturday, at Amit's place…" Jiya hesitantly confessed.

"If you weren't my childhood friend, I would have ripped your hair off for talking shit about my husband. Now, get lost from here", Kanika yelled, lunging towards Jiya.

But Jiya opened her phone and showed Kanika the cozy pictures she clicked with Kunal and smirked.

"How about this? Saturday night…" Jiya showed her the pictures from her phone gallery.

"Fucking bitch!" Kanika blasted, thrusting the phone back at Jiya. She pushed Jiya out of her house. She slammed door behind her and screamed "Get out of my life! Get out!". She sobbed and sat down by the door. She looked at the decorations she just did. In a fit of anger she got up and she started wrecking all the decorations for her dinner with Kunal. She broke down in tears, wondering if she should trust Kunal or Jiya.

After a while Kunal enters the room, he has just returned from work. He kept his bag on the couch, wallet on the table and sat down on the couch turning on the TV. Kanika and Kunal are sitting on both the ends of couch and Kanika is paying no heed to Kunal, she got up and sat on a different couch seat. "Could you bring food? I am hungry." Kunal demanded. Kanika didn't pay any attention. Kunal in frustration calls her out. "Are you listening?", Kunal inquired. Kanika didn't budge. "Hello, Bring some food?", Kunal raised his voice. "It's in the refrigerator", Kanika snaps back at Kunal and gets up to go inside. "What's this drama? What the fuck is with your attitude?", Kunal questioned. "Drama? What the hell are YOU doing?", Kanika retorted. "What am I doing?", Kunal asked in frustration. "Jiya was here today and she told me that you slept with her." Kanika revealed and tried to test him. "Oh God! You know how she is? Right? She is crazy. She talks anything, don't come under her influence", Kunal maneuvered Kanika by reminding her of Jiya's nature. "Oh is that so? Then are these pictures also lying?", Kanika interrogated Kunal. "Which Pictures?", Kunal snapped and pretended to not recall. "Here see this! You are holding her! What the hell? What are you doing?", Kanika grilled Kunal. Kunal was speechless. "Who am I supposed to trust? These pictures or you?", Kanika interrogated Kunal. "Trust me!! I am doing everything to keep this relationship.", Kunal pleaded and reminded Kanika. "I don't think so! Because It's our anniversary and you forgot!", Kanika blamed Kunal and stormed to her bedroom. Kunal tried to stop her but she slammed the door on his face leaving him flabbergasted. Kunal didn't have any cards to play now.

***

The next day, Kanika entered the classroom and seemed gloomy for the morning. All the students were settling down as she entered and waited for further instructions from her. Kanika thought for a while about the last nights fight with Kunal but then gathered herself and the class around her in a wide circle. "Today, we will do a story-telling session that evokes a certain emotion in you. Any volunteers? Kanika asked.

"I'll.. ", Sunaina excitedly raised her hand. Hiten intervenes with a heavy voice and overlaps Sunaina, "I will go!". Hiten walks with bhai style, Dabangg music playing in background and is already at the center stage. He sniffs like bhai and gets in his story telling mode.

"Today I am going to regale you with a tale of courage, integrity and will power!! This story is one from my many amazing stories. This was when I was drinking my johnny walker blue label with imarti and peanuts with my friends on my terrace. Then with my sexy blue eagle eyes I saw a big bulky bull entering our street and charging in the direction of a small kid. Kid started running and bull chasing him. Looking at that I thought of saving that kid and the moment that bull approached my house I jumped from my terrace in front of the bull and held by his horns and pushed him back!" All are laughing at his made up story but he still continues. "The bull started going back and was scared of me! The bull finally grunted I am sorry Master Hiten, in his language and bowed to me and left! All the people started chanting my name and the kid thanked me for saving my life!" Gully ka dada kaun! Hiten aur Kaun! Is gully me rehna hai toh Hiten hiten Kehna hai"

Everyone started laughing and chanting the slogans and Kanika calmed them down", Okay! Wonderful!" Kanika exclaimed! "So this story evokes bravery in you. Great! Hard to believe but it serves the purpose. Sunaina now you go!" Kanika asked Sunaina to come forward.

Hiten took his place and Sunaina walked in place of him.

"Okay. So, this happened when I was living in Delhi. I was on the Metro one day when I noticed this Muslim Maulana type man. I mean, I knew that he was a Muslim because he was wearing the typical attire— had the big beard, something in eyes as well as that suit. What do they call it?" Sunaina asked, looking at Azim.

"They call suit *Pathani* and Kohl in eyes ", Azim responded .

"Oh, yeah! That's what it's called." Sunaina repeated what Azim had just said. "He was wearing that along with a greenish blackish Pathani suit. Anyway, the point is that he was very clearly a Muslim guy. He was sitting there in the Metro talking to these teenage children. For some reason, I felt that he was trying to brainwash those children. It felt like he was trying to indoctrinate them. He was showing some videos on his phone and was yelling something at them. But I could tell this wasn't just angry yelling. I knew it was something political - I heard one of the children say what he was saying was right and that they needed to have an answer. So, I knew something was going on and began eavesdropping on their conversation... "

Sunaina trailed off. A very long and awkward pause filled the room. No one had any idea about what they should say after hearing this. Azim looked really offended after hearing Sunaina's story.

"This evoked emotion of fear and anger in me. I guess that's it", Sunaina concluded as she sat down.

"Okay, I understand that you can be afraid experiencing something like this. But what made you think that person was Muslim? That could've just been any person and not particularly a Muslim, you know?" Kanika reasoned.

"Oh! I'm pretty sure he was a Muslim. He was wearing that pathani suit, had a big beard and kohl around his eyes." Sunaina retorted.

"He may have fit your stereotypical description of a Muslim man, but he could've been anyone. Hell, he might not even be a Muslim. Sometimes what we see isn't really the truth", Kanika enlightened and made them understand.

Sunaina took it personally and remained quiet. There was another long pause and silence in the room.

Finally, Kanika looked at her watch and said, "Anyway, Thank you, guys. This was a brilliant start. Let's take a break now."

The students went to their seats to get their bags. Some of them took out their phones, while some went to get a drink of water. Others relaxed.

Kanika stopped Jheel and inquired, "Jheel? I had almost forgotten to ask you. Before you go…I think you haven't paid your fees yet."

"Oh! I'm sorry. My mom was supposed to give it to you", Jheel replied. "Oh! I don't think she gave it to me. Will you remind her of that?" "Sure!"..

***

In the women's bathroom, Sunaina was busy applying her make up when Jheel entered.

"Hey, did I say anything wrong?" Sunaina asked. "When?" Jheel questioned.

"Just before the break. The story I was telling..." Sunaina reminded. "Well, to be honest, it's quite a sensitive topic", Jheel explained.

"Yes, I know. But I don't think I said anything wrong about the community. I just said what I had seen that day."

"That's fine but you need to be careful about what you're saying. Also, Kanika was right. You cannot stereotype an entire community based on what they wear or how they appear or how just one man looks. Anyways, forget about what happened. Let's get back to class", Jheel pacified, trying to make Sunaina feel better.

***

While inside the studio Azim and Anant were chit chatting. "I had fun listening to the stories", Anant expressed.

"Yeah. But now, we must remember all the details. These exercises are getting tough", Azim exclaimed. Hiten approached both in excitement to share some interesting incident. Hiten swayed towards them in Salman Bhai's style.

"Hey, leave all this aside. I'll tell you a really, really hot and exciting story…" Hiten lured them. He beckoned Azim and Anant closer and whispered, "Yesterday, I wanted to ask Kanika Ma'am about something. So, I went to her office after class … and I saw… Kunal and ma'am were in the middle of getting it on, if you know what I mean. Hot and heavy. I didn't want to disturb them, but unfortunately the door made a noise." Hiten clicked his tongue in a wolfish whistle. "By the way, ma'am is not that bad."

Anant and Azim recoiled in embarrassment at Hiten's attitude.

"Anant, you beware of Kunal. Have you seen how Kunal is eyeing your item - Sunaina?" Hiten warned.

"First of all, please don't call her an item. Give her some respect — she's a woman not an object.", Anant snapped at Hiten.

"You are a disgusting person, Hiten. Everything you say is disgusting. Looks like your mind is filled with shit.", Anant said, incensed. "I'm leaving."

"Go, go! Go jack off!" Hiten yelled after him. Slowly

***

The students assembled in the classroom after the break. Anant and Sunaina stood six feet apart, facing each other. They prepared themselves for the repetition exercise. They were looking into each other's eyes, observing one another's behavior. They smiled and blushed but managed not to break eye contact. They had the connection established and both were on the verge of getting their impulses to surface. It came naturally to them.

"Your eyes are very beautiful", Anant complimented Sunaina and openly confessed his long hidden feelings for her.

"My eyes are very beautiful?" Sunaina asked him in surprise taking in what he just said. "Your eyes are very beautiful", Anant repeated and assured her.

"My eyes are very beautiful?" Sunaina questioned him again.

"Yes, your eyes are very beautiful", Anant confirmed.

"My eyes are very beautiful?", Sunaina seductively asked again taking a step towards Anant.

"When you talk like this… I feel some sensations in my body.", Anant confessed.

"You feel sensations inside of you?", Sunaina laughed it out.

"Yes. I feel sensations in my body", Anant assured feeling every bit of it.

"Where do you feel sensations in body?" Sunaina quizzed Anant.

Anant feels shy and embarrassing.

"I feel like...", Anant tried expressing his feelings upfront without holding back anything but couldn't say no more.

"Oh… So, you feel like kissing me now?" Sunaina laughed at his statement. "Yes, I do feel like kissing you", Anant repeated in confidence.

Sunaina was aroused. "Do you really feel like kissing me?"

"Yes…" Anant was provoked and moved closer.

"Then do it.." Sunaina challenged him mockingly, wanted to check if he does it and moved closer to Anant. They kept moving closer to each other. They were just inches away from one another when Kanika stood up to interrupt them.

"Oh, don't stop now", the class exclaimed and groaned in disappointment wanting to see some kissing in the class.

"No, no, no! Stop! I told you no physical contact in the exercise", Kanika stopped and reminded them. Anant and Sunaina jerked apart and went back to their places.

"I know guys! You are disappointed. But this is what happens when you connect with your partner and work off their behavior.", Kanika explained. "This is amazing guys. You were connected and your impulses were genuine. Good Job!". Kanika complimented.

Sunaina and Anant nodded in acknowledgement and headed to their seats. Everyone packed their bags and started heading out the studio.

***

"So, what are you going to do now?" Anant asked. "Nothing much… I'll just go home", Sunaina pretended.

"Okay…" Anant blushed and smiled, not knowing what to say. There was an awkward silence between them.

"Will you go out for a coffee with me?" Sunaina asked.

"No… I mean, why not?" Anant replied with a glint in his eyes, and his lips parted in a smile. As Sunaina walked in front of him, Anant jumped with joy expressing his victory coffee date.

Chapter 4

A corner house to the busy street. Azim's father is sitting in the living room reading newspaper. "Azim, I asked you to get the papers from the upper shelf of the cupboard, and you still haven't done it... you're so irresponsible", Azim's father ordered from the living room of his home.

"Yeah, I'll get them now", he said annoyingly, and walked to his dad's study. He reached for the old paper file on the top shelf. His hands groped on the shelf and found a box. Curious, he shook the box gently and heard a tinkle and a jingle. Cautiously, he brought the box down and wiped the dust from it with his palm. It was stuck and was not easy to open. When he finally got it to open, he saw his mother's cosmetics and the anklets (Ghungroo) that she used for her dance. He forgot about the file and walked back to his room carrying the box close to his chest.

Azim closed the door of his room and removed the contents of the box one by one and laid it in a line on his bed. His mother's anklets, some photographs, cosmetics like *bindi,* mascara, and lipstick; a colorful diaphanous *dupatta* and some other scarves she used for her dance. When he was a kid, his mother used to explain him about the dances. Her Kathak performances. He went back in time.

Azim was in the audience, watching his mom perform. When her dance performance ended, everyone started to clap and cheer for her. She bowed to the audience and walked backstage, where Azim met her.

"Ammi, what a performance! Everyone went crazy over it..." Azim complimented her. "Did you watch?" his mom asked.

"Yes!"

"I thought you couldn't make it. Did you have fun?"

"Yes, yes...a lot of fun...I am proud of you", Azim complimented and kissed his mother on the forehead.

"Abba didn't know, right? Didn't you come across anyone familiar on the way?" his mom asked, worried.

"No, Ammi...I tip-toed out of the house and came here...and no one saw me", he comforted her. "You are such a great dancer. I want to dance like you too."

"Yeah, sure...let's go now. Abba will come home soon; we need to get home before him."

After reminiscing, Azim took out her photograph from the box. He stuck it at the edge of his mirror and tried to look like his mom. He even applied some makeup, tied her *dupatta* around his waist, wore her anklets and began to dance, feeling the presence of his mother with him. His mind once again went to the past.

Azim and his mother entered the living room from the front door and noticed Azim's father sitting on the chair. His expression was unreadable. Both halted in the doorway.

"Is the nuisance done?" his father asked sternly. "What are you saying?" his mother asked.

Azim's father showed them the pictures of her dancing.

After waiting for his paper file, Azim's father heard the sound of anklets from Azim's room. Azim's father entered the room and saw Azim in the attire and was shocked looking at him. Azim was in deep thoughts.

"What have you done to your face?", His father shouted. "Do you think of yourself as a woman? Take it all out. You are a man...a MAN! Do you want to make me feel ashamed in front of the world like your mom? Do you want to be like your mother? A dancer?" his father raged.

"Yes, I want to become like her. Not like you", Azim replied in angst. "Don't raise your voice", his father commanded and slapped Azim for his retort. Azim's father left leaving Azim in disheveled state.

Azim untied the *dupatta* and began wiping his makeup with it, all the while looking at his mother's picture.

* * *

Kanika was in her office getting ready for class when she heard a knock on the door. She looked up to see a woman at the door.

"Hi, I am Neha, Jheel's mother", Neha introduced herself. "Oh, hi. Please come in... Have a seat." Kanika welcomed Neha.

"Jheel talked to me about the fees yesterday", Neha reminded, and took an envelope out of her bag.

"Yeah, I reminded her about the fee", Kanika mentioned.

"Here, this is the fee for her class", Neha said, handing the envelope to

Kanika.

Kanika took the money from the envelope and counted it. She verified and said, "I think it falls short by five thousand rupees."

"I will pay the rest of the money by next month, is that okay?" Neha asked.

"No problem, ma'am. Anyway, I'm really glad Jheel has parents like you, who understand and support their kid at such a young age. I wish everyone's parents were like that." Kanika complimented Neha.

"Not her dad, just me", Neha proudly mentioned, and went on to explain her situation to Kanika. "I'm supporting her all by myself. My husband never cared for us. I am divorced and I want to make her an independent woman like me, who can look after herself." Neha took a moment to compose herself and exclaimed, "I'm sorry, I've been talking too much…". Though she was sharing too much with Kanika, there was a sense of pride in her voice when she talked about how she wanted to raise her daughter.

This triggered Kanika into a self-realization about her own life. She wasn't happy with where she and her life with Kunal was going. Kanika had always wanted to take control of her own life, but she never found the courage to do so. She was inspired by Neha's words, and thought that she could also do everything on her own, without anyone's help.

"What you are doing as a single mother is great. You inspire me.", Kanika complimented smiling at her.

They shook hands and Neha left the office. Kanika sat in her office, deep in thought about her life before getting back to work.

***

Kanika entered the studio with enthusiasm and announced. "Guys, we will be playing the *dog and the bone* game. I hope everyone knows this game", Kanika quizzed.

"What kind of game is this?" Anant asked.

"Hey, I know how to play this. I used to play it as a kid", Ragini boasted.

"Okay then, Ragini will play the game with me and show the rest. Ragini, you are the captain of the first team, and I will be the captain of the other. Choose your team", Kanika instructed.

"Anant", Ragini called. "Jheel", Kanika continued.

Ragini called out Azim's name.

It was Kanika's turn to choose. "Hiten", she said. "Kunal", Ragini continued.

"Sunaina", Kanika ended by choosing the last person in her team. "Ragini and I will go first to show you how it's played. Let's start."

Kanika used hula-hoop prop for the circle and placed a soft toy in the center to serve as the bone. Both the teams faced each other. Kanika went back to the group and took the starting stance; Ragini did the same.

Kunal started to count down for the game. "3… 2… 1… Go!"

Kanika and Ragini rushed towards the bone and circled around it, trying to figure out the best way to pick up the bone and run away. "Kanika! Kanika! Kanika!", Kanika's team cheered for her. "Ragini! Ragini!", cheered Ragini's team as they played. "Kallo!! Kallo!! (Blacky! Blacky!)", Hiten shouted. Suddenly, Kanika grabbed the bone and raced back to join her team evading Ragini's grasp.

"See, I'm going to make you lose", Hiten mocked Ragini aggressively. Ragini was pissed that she lost the game, but her team consoled her.

"Did everyone understand the game?" Kanika asked. "You have to steal the bone and run away without letting the opponent catch you."

Everyone nodded.

"Next up is Sunaina from my team." Kanika excitedly chose Sunaina.

"I will go!", Anant said to Ragini.

"Okay! It's going to be Anant from my side." Ragini confirmed.

Sunaina took her stance. Hiten leaned in and whispered something into Sunaina's ear. She nodded and smiled. She walked towards Anant. Slowly and seductively, adjusting her blouse, looking straight into Anant's eyes. Anant was mesmerized by her beauty, which hypnotized him. Sunaina purposefully showed her cleavage to Anant. Anant got aroused the moment he noticed it and was just looking at it amorously. Sunaina took this opportunity to grab the bone and left quickly before he could react.

"What the hell, Anant?" Ragini yelled at him. "All men are the same. A woman gives you some attention, and you forget the world around you." Ragini blamed and complained.

Kanika's team won yet again. Hiten shouted with joy. The team scores were 2-0.

"Kunal from my side", Ragini called out on Kunal. "Jheel", Kanika retorted.

They both started to move towards the bone cautiously once the countdown was done. Kunal lifted the bone easily, disappointing Jheel. He tried to give her the bone, but she refused it. He insisted she take it. Hiten was mad, but Ragini was happy.

"We are back in the game, fucker!" It was now Ragini's turn to mock Hiten. "It's my turn now. I'll show you what I'm capable of", Hiten retorted.

"Azim, come on. Show him how it's done", Ragini called out to Azim and encouraged him to defeat Hiten.

Azim walked towards the bone a bit scared. He quickly picked the bone and turned back to run. Hiten grabbed his hand and dragged Azim to his own team, along with the bone. Ragini was mad and started to yell at Hiten. Everyone, on the other hand, was laughing excitedly. Azim dropped the bone and Hiten grabbed it and tore it into pieces, declaring himself a winner. The innards of the soft toy settled on the floor like discarded tissue.

"I am a fan of Salman, the Superman!" Hiten screamed triumphantly. He danced and made fun of Ragini. After his mini celebration, everyone calmed him down. Ragini remained furious.

"Awesome, you guys! This was a good game, right? Do you know why we play these games? Because they keep us liberated, away from our mind and thoughts...in the moment..." Kanika paused before continuing. "We let go of all the barriers and restrictions, and we indulge completely in the present. Just like Hiten did", she praised, pointing at Hiten.

"Now, let's take our places. Kunal will tell us his story and we must remember it. So, listen carefully. Okay?" Kunal took center stage while Kanika sat with the students.

"My name is Kanika Arora", Kunal said, scratching his head and grinning. He was imitating his wife for the exercise. "My husband is supposed to do this monologue about me but, he really doesn't know… I live in Versova, Andheri. I…umm…I'm the director of the Kalamanch Theater group and I teach a bunch of classes like…" he stuttered for a bit before continuing, "…I have been interested in teaching creative drama classes for adults and now, I'm finally doing it. I love reading plays and novels; my favorite playwright is…who is it?" Kunal tried to remember but couldn't. "…I don't know I forgot that. I love kids; I like to play with my stepdaughter a lot… In the nights, when I am supposed to give time to my husband…" Kunal trailed off, chuckling sarcastically. "I'm a foodie but not a great cook. Ask my husband, he'll tell you." Kunal finished, laughing at himself.

Kanika's facial expression changed from happy to awkward as Kunal went through the impersonation exercise. She headed for the stage.

"Thank you Kunal. That's enough", Kanika stopped Kunal before he lets out their personal life more into light. She turned to the students. "So guys, we need to understand the life of our partners through our lens to know more about their perspective. You need to come up here and tell their stories as if you are them. Okay?" Kanika explained.

While the students nodded, some looked skeptical about sharing intimate details of their lives on stage. Now let's do the emotion evoking exercise Kanika called out Azim's name.

Azim stood up from his seat and walked towards the center stage facing the rest of his classmates, who were listening intently. Azim then started to talk…

"My best friend… The last time we made a plan, it was great. We went

to visit Shimla during the summer vacation. We had a lot of fun —
paragliding, river rafting, and trekking. We drank alcohol and smoked
a lot without anyone noticing. I don't even remember how the days
passed in that intoxication. I was very happy!"

Azim paused. His face was sincere, and everyone noticed that he was
really into the story he was narrating. "I don't know what happened but
after returning from the trip, he stopped contacting me and started to
ignore me. When I tried to call him, I realized that he had blocked my
phone number too. And then… one day I stopped him between classes
to have a conversation, but he got angry and slapped me, saying not to
touch him ever again." He closed his eyes, reliving the painful incident.

"I was so stunned at his behavior that I couldn't say anything. I felt so
embarrassed in front of everyone that I started crying. But he walked
away like he didn't care. I never spoke to him after that incident. I don't
know… what happened between us. Years of our friendship was broken
in a snap. I really miss him." This story evokes an emotion of sadness
in me.

Everyone in the class seemed to understand Azim's sorrow. "Your story
was good, Azim. If you don't mind me asking, how long have you guys
not talked to each other?" Kanika asked.

"It's been five years. We haven't been in touch." Azim answered.

"I think you should reconnect." Kanika suggested.

"Yeah, I guess…" Azim exclaimed gloomily.

"Alright guys", Kanika directed the class to take a break. "This is all
very good. Let's take a ten-minute break."

***

Kanika was stacking books on the shelves in her office, when Jheel knocked and entered.

"Ma'am, did you call me?" Jheel asked. "Jheel...come, yes. Please take a seat", Kanika welcomed. "I think my mom paid the fee, right?" Jheel mentioned thinking she was called for the fees.

"Yeah, yeah. She did, this morning." Kanika communicated.

"Cool, then", Jheel said, wondering what Kanika might have called her for. "How are the classes going?" Kanika inquired.

"Very well, but I wonder when we get to do some real acting." Jheel expressed her thoughts concerning the acting process.

"Real acting? You are getting ready to do real acting...and I think you are doing a great job." Kanika complimented Jheel.

"Really?" Jheel asked with excitement.

"Yes, you are very observant and committed to the classes. And you are doing really well." Kanika smiled and assured her.

"Thanks. I really appreciate it."

"I met your mother today, and I must say, you are lucky to have her. She is a great mother."

"Yes, I am proud of her. She always gives me the best...whatever I need." Jheel validated.

"I am really inspired by her..." Kanika praised her mother. She paused. "I have a daughter, too. I mean stepdaughter; she is almost your age. We both have a strong bond."

"Oh, that's nice."

"You remind me of her. Please stop by if there is anything you want to discuss. My doors are always open."

"That's so thoughtful of you. Thank you, ma'am." Jheel left the office with a smile on her face.

Chapter 5

Anant and Sunaina arrived at Kalamanch early the next day. As soon as they entered the studio, Anant got bolder and pinned her against the wall. Soon they were kissing, and their hands were all over the other's body. Anant slipped his hands under Sunaina's skirt.

"Ahh..Hhhey, slow down! Your ring is pricking me", Sunaina cried out and stopped Anant. "Okay, I'll use my other hand", Anant mentioned.

"Stop! Stop! Someone may walk in." Sunaina tried to wriggle away.

"Oh! C'mon, no one comes this early.", Anant persuaded.

"Please stop baby!" Sunaina requested.

"Since the day I met you. I have always thought about you, while I was in the shower", Anant seduced Sunaina. "Oh is it? Even I was thinking of you at night on my bed.", Sunaina panted. "Do you wanna do it. Let's go into the restroom", Anant persuaded Sunaina. "Have you gone mad? No way", Sunaina denied.

"Just for few seconds. Please!", Anant insisted and was adamant.

Sunaina heard someone walking towards the studio. "What was that?" Sunaina pulled away and looked towards the studio entrance door. She slipped away and hurried into the ladies restroom. Anant straightened up and Ragini turned the corner and gave a yelp when she was going to bump Sunaina at the door she but stopped herself. Sunaina passed her and Ragini entered the studio. As she found Anant adjusting himself and a mark of lipstick on his face, Ragini gave a disgusted look, turned back, and proceeded towards her seat.

"*Namastey* Ms. Ragini", Anant greeted and maneuvered Ragini. Ragini acknowledged but knew what was going on between them.

Gradually all the students were present in the studio, some doing acting exercises like stretching, voice modulation, movement etc. Kanika entered the studio and was happy to see the students working on their craft. "Okay guys, we're going to start with the intros. Remember we spoke about it a while ago, where Kunal did my introduction? I hope everyone remembers their partner's intros. Anant, let's begin with you", Kanika pointed him out excitedly.

Anant was going through his large notebook. Anant got up and went into the prep room. Everyone was patiently waiting for Anant to come out. Anant takes a step out of the prep room totally with a new personality. He walks like a super model and takes his place at the center stage. All are excited to see Anant's behavior. Some start shouting and hooting "Anant! Anant!". Anant stops and takes a compact in hand and starts applying it on his face in Sunaina's style. Everyone is enjoying Anant's actions. Hiten whistles at him. Sunaina too is enjoying and somewhat embarrassed. After applying the make up Anant takes a breath.

"Hi my name iz Sunaina." Anant started off speaking in English, however it sounded like Chinese to everyone and some started laughing at him. Anant stopped for a moment and gathered back his courage. Anant with confidence started again. My name is Sunaina and I am 26 years old, I am from New Delhi and living in Bandra since 6 months. My father is a top ranked Military officer in Indian Army and my Mother was a big time Bhojpuri actress. I myself am a Super Model and I do ads for beauty products as you can see, I am very beautiful. Anant looks at Sunaina for her acceptance and Sunaina looks back at him with a smile, acknowledging it. Anant continues, "It's not just the outer appearance that is beautiful but also my heart is beautiful. I am not biased to anyone. I don't differentiate between dark or fair, young or old, native or foreigner, from Belapur or Bandra, short or tall I just don't care at all. Before coming here, my heart was broken by a stupid guy and he hurt me real bad. However now I feel like I have found the one for whom I was looking for my whole life. My soulmate! Should I tell who that lucky guy is?", Anant teasingly looks at Sunaina and she shyly gestures him to not say it. Anant acknowledges this and moves on with saying, "Let it be. Save it for the next time!".

"That was good, Anant", Kanika commended him. "I see a lot of growth in you. You really portrayed characteristics and behavior very well today. Keep up the good work! I am proud of you."

"*Dhanyawaad* ma'am." He thanked her in Hindi. Anant feeling confident after hearing the compliments and suddenly he remembers a voice that destroyed his confidence. "You are good for nothing!", the voice echoed in his head repeatedly. It was his Ex-Wife Sonali who cursed him using these words.

Anant reminisces him buying a watch for Sonali for her 25th Birthday, excited he enters a watch store and browses through array of watches. The salesperson approaches Anant and asks, "Hello! What are you looking for?"

"This is the watch shop right?", Anant inquired. "Yes! But you have come to a wrong store. It's way above your standards!", Hearing this the store manager intervenes and scolds the salesperson because he handled customer improperly.

The manager shows Anant number of watches and also the best-selling watch at their store. Anant gets his eye on one of the bestselling watches and wishes to buy it for Sonali on her Birthday. "How much is this watch for?", Anant inquired. "Ten thousand rupees.", Manager responded. Anant was taken aback by the price as it was half of his monthly pay check. Reading Anant's expression the Manager offers Anant a rebate on the watch.

Anant happily buys the watch thinking Sonali would love it and leaves for the Birthday Party of Sonali at their place.

The apartment is decorated with flowers and balloons, people are enjoying the party, Anant comes to the apartment and looks for Sonali but she is nowhere to find. Anant asks one of Sonali's friend but she hesitates to tell him about her. Looking for Sonali in the crowded apartment Anant searches the bedroom, kitchen but still she is nowhere to be found and finally Anant heads to the restroom for taking a leak and surprisingly he finds Sonali with Rohan his best friend in it. Shocked at them, Anant questions, "What are you guys doing here?". Rohan deflects by laughing it off and saying, "Oh! I wasn't able to turn this tap off!". Anan sarcastically replied, "I think I was the one from small town". Sonali intervenes, "Hey Anant Where is your ring? Are you hitting on your colleagues at office?". Anant is startled by it and assures her that He took off the ring while washing his face and forgot to put it on! They all leave the restroom and start enjoying the party. After a while all gather to see Sonali's gifts as she is opening them one by one. She finally gets to the gift of Anant and opens it up in excitement. Her face turns sad to angry as she finds out it's a watch of some local brand. She is angry at the gift, and she bursts out in anger. "What the hell is this? You were supposed to give me an iPhone 5". She throws the gift on Anant in front of all of the guests and yells at him, "You are good for nothing! Loser!" Storms to her room. Anant is embarrassed and is hurt.

Azim snaps fingers in front of Anant and brings him back in the present. "Hey brother! You were good. There is good improvement in you". Anant gathers himself and responds to Azim, "Thank you Azim Bhai. You guys inspire me."

Hiten swaggered in, whistling, and behaving as if he had achieved something big. He was whistling the tune of the popular Hindi song, *Bheege hoth tere.*"Oh, Mr. Anant, how are you doing? I have something I need to show you. Could you please come here?" Hiten lured him.

Not wishing to interact with Hiten, Azim left the room.

"So, tell me, What do you want to show me?" Anant asked.

"Take a look at this couple's make out session", Hiten said creating a hype, and beckoned Anant closer.

"No, thank you. I am not a voyeur", Anant ignored, but Hiten held his arm and pulled him closer.

"Believe me, this is interesting", Hiten said, menacingly.

Anant watched the video with mounting horror. What was a romantic interlude between him and Sunaina looked crass and distasteful when watched as a video.

"Please delete this video at once", Anant pleaded. "What's the hurry? Watch the whole thing", Hiten urged.

"Please, delete this video. Please don't pass it around to others. I'm begging you", Anant pleaded.

"Oh no! Things like this, these beautiful moments are not meant to be deleted. They are saved and cherished", Hiten boasted.

"Please Hiten. I'll do anything you ask. What do you want?" Anant asked.

"Well, here's the thing. I am not greedy for money. But that ring of yours is very beautiful. Also, you don't seem to have a need for it. Am I right?" Hiten asked.

Anant looked at his ring and felt very disturbed. "Hiten, what are you saying? I cannot give this to you. It's my promise to someone.", Anant reasoned and pleaded.

"What is a wedding ring when there is no marriage anymore? I cannot delete this as well, Mr. Anant", Hiten cautioned.

"Bro, I can pay you the value of the ring. We can get it appraised", Anant suggested.

***

"It's not about money my Romeo. I want the Taj Mahal. A symbol of your love." Hiten demanded.

As Hiten said it, Anant went through inner turmoil. He kept thinking about his promise and was in a dilemma. He finally gave in and decided to give the ring to Hiten. He struggled to get the ring off his finger.

Hiten looking at his attempt, hurriedly grabbed his hand and pried the ring out of Anant's hand. "Thank you so very much", Hiten thanked mocking him. Anant was furious at Hiten, He gathered courage and threatened, "But now, you need to delete that video", Anant demanded. Hiten looked at Anant in demeaning way and deleted the video as Anant watched him.

Anant felt relieved but also disgusted by Hiten's actions. "You are a very dirty and perverted person", Anant thrashed at Hiten and rushed out of the studio.

"Thank you, thank you", Hiten echoed. And there was nothing more to be said.

***

After the break, Kanika started the exercise with Hiten.

"Hey guys, let's get started now. Hiten, you go first", Kanika announced.

Hiten got up and headed to the stage. He was very excited and showed his love for Bollywood by placing his glasses on the back of his shirt collar like Salman Khan in the movie *Dabangg*. He kept his *Dabangg* style going.

"My best friend! We had a great plan. To visit Shimla! To escape our mundane life and do something spicy and hot in the cold of Shimla. We did a lot of fun activities like.. Fuck!!!! Sorry! flying in the air with parachutes…We drank cum.. sorry alcohol…smoked weed and shit!! Sloshed drunk we did so many naughty shenanigans in each other's arms, legs and on top of each other.. ooohh!! I don't know who was on top but I liked it" Hearing this mockery Azim is embarrassed and humiliated. Rest all were finding it funny in the beginning but soon realized that it was way out of the limits. Hiten continued I", But after coming back from the trip, My best friend stopped talking to me! OMG and I tried to ask him Why?? Then he slapped on my Ass and said not to touch bitch! I was so hard.. oh Sorry Hurt! I cried like a pussy and screamed give me an O! and ran home!". Kanika stopped Hiten from going further and shut him off. Azim is devastated, humiliated and angry at Hiten's slurs, we can see that in his eyes.

"Alright guys, enough is enough. Please don't use these Exercises as a chance to butcher your classmates. Please have some understanding and respect for each other", Kanika reminded. "Okay guys, let's wrap up. That's all for today. We'll continue this tomorrow." She exited the room. The others followed suit, muttering among themselves about how offensive Hiten had been.

Anant gestured to Sunaina that he would join her later and walked up to Azim. Ragini was consoling him, but she left when she saw Anant approaching, figuring that he would be better at handling Azim.

"I've had enough of Hiten's antics. I'm going to beat him up. I'll teach him a lesson after everyone leaves", Anant bravely admitted.

"Today he's going to get it!" Azim replied.

Hiten was nonchalantly packing his stuff in his bag and trying to act casual after his speech.

"Hold on a second, son! Today you're going to learn a lesson", Anant challenged Hiten. "Oh, shut up! You dumb fuck! Get lost or I'll leak the video", Hiten replied.

"Wait! You didn't delete the video? I saw you doing it", Anant asked, shocked and terrified.

"Nope." Hiten laughed. "What video?" Azim asked.

"Go ahead. Tell him", Hiten taunted. "Or shall I tell him?" "No, no, please don't. I beg you", Anant pleaded.

"Then get lost." Hiten scared Anant away. "Loser."

Anant looked at Azim apologetically and left the room.

"Did you have something to tell me, Azim?" Hiten mocked Azim.

***

Without saying anything Azim charged towards Hiten and kicks him, Hiten in return lunges onto Azim and they start pushing each other, then they get into shoulder tackle mode, Hiten parries one hand and plants a knee kick on Azim's stomach due to which Azim falls on the ground, Hiten tries to sit on him to plant punches but Azim locks his one leg in scissor and pushes him over and then falls beside him and now Azim gets on top of him, they both try to hit each other, Hiten rolls Azim over and gets on top of Azim and they both are pushing and blocking each other, while applying force their eyes get lock They both connect with each other while looking in each other's eyes and come closer slowly applying forces. Hiten suddenly plants a peck on Azim's lips, and held back for a while and again starts kissing him. The force is over and they start kissing hard. And suddenly Hiten realizes and gets up takes a moment, feels disgusted of what he just did and spits on Azim. Hiten leaves in disgust. Azim is on the floor thinking about the whole situation wiping his face and is very confused of what just happened. Blackout

Chapter 6

Chilling music beats coming from a bedroom, Sunaina just walked out of the shower and threw her towel on the bed. She had put out her outfit for the day. After she was dressed, she put on her makeup. Looking herself in the mirror, she winked and left for the class. When she opened her front door, she found Nic standing there. She heaved a deep sigh about having to deal with him again.

"Why the hell are you here?" Sunaina asked.

"I saw you third time at the coffee shop with that same loser", Nic interrogated. "So? Why do you care? And stop following me around", Sunaina warned and started walking. "You've really dropped your standards now, haven't you?" Nic taunted. As she heard it, she thought about it for a second whether Nic was saying the truth. However, she shrugged off that thought and snapped at Nic, "At least he's not an abusive, control freak like you".

"Listen, I have changed! I've already apologized 506 times. This is 507th. I'm sorry!" Nic reminded and convinced Sunaina.

"Now add my 507th time saying no to you. I've made up my mind. Get the fuck out of my life", Sunaina rejected him.

"Okay, whether you forgive me or not, I don't care. But do not humiliate me by making that loser your new boyfriend", Nic suggested.

Sunaina ignored him but still thought about what Nic said to her about Anant. She hurried away disappearing in the busy street. She unknowingly walked past Ragini who was lost in her own thoughts.

A stranger on a bicycle swung close to Ragini and began taunting her. "Hey, Blackie maid! Get out of the way", the cyclist yelled.

He commented on her dark skin tone. Ragini curses back at him saying "Get the fuck out of here, else I will beat the hell out of you." He scurries away.

Ragini hearing his taunt thinks back to the time she was interviewing for a cabin crew job. Without any interview they told her that she had failed their initial screening. Ragini challenged the interviewers and questioned about their biased values towards tan colored people.

***

All the students were in the studio working on their craft. Kanika entered with a zest, "Alright guys! I have something for you", Kanika announced excitedly. "Each one of you will come up with a small skit of your own. You are free to choose your classmates and give them any character you want in your skit. Sounds good? Before you guys dive into preparing your skit lets hear out Jheel's monologue story."

Jheel stood in front of the classroom in a shirt, formal pants, and dorky glasses. She was the female version of Anant. She walked forward uncomfortably, like Anant. It made everyone giggle.

"Hi, my name is Anant Singh Thakur. I'm 30 years old, but I look younger than I am. I was born and raised in Shahjahanpur which is in Uttar Pradesh. My father, Brijesh Singh Thakur is a shop…" She paused. She sounded weird while talking in Hindi to herself and everyone was laughing with her. Then she continued in English.

"He is the owner of Roli bookstore. My mother, Roli Singh Thakur is a housewife. My mom is the closest to me and the most loving person in my life. She supports me in everything I've ever wanted to do. I'm here now in front of you all because of her. Today, who I am is because of my mother and her prayers. She prays to Lord Krishna. She is a big believer in his powers", Jheel continued.

Jheel saw acceptance in Anant's eyes which motivated her to continue.

"My mother taught me to be truthful and simple. In Mumbai, I live alone as I am a divorcee…" Jheel noticed Anant tensing and signaling her to change the topic.

"It wasn't my fault that our marriage did not last. She cheated on me. She also pushed my mother out of my life, that bi…" Jheel was agitated saying these but then stopped.

Anant looked visibly upset.

Jheel cleared her throat. "I can't believe how some people can do that to such a kind- hearted individual."

"Stay on track, Jheel", Kanika guided, interrupting Jheel's monologue. "I'm sorry ma'am", Jheel replied.

She paused to gather her thoughts together. "I love old Hindi songs like Jheel. Kishore Kumar is my favorite singer." She then picked up the guitar and started singing the song *Bheegi Bheegi Raaton Mein.*

Anant grooved to the beat, while the others joined and cheered.

***

After Jheel's intro about Anant, the class split into different teams for the next exercise. Some began planning their skits while another group helped each other with their scripts.

Azim was busy writing his script in the classroom. Anant left to get something to eat. Sunaina was doing her stretches in the corner. Kunal was eating his salad and watching her. Kunal wanted to talk to Sunaina but wanted to get rid of Azim before he did so.

"What happened? You are not having lunch today?" Kunal asked. "No... don't feel like having it", Azim replied.

"You shouldn't skip your lunch. It is unhealthy. Go get something to eat", Kunal insisted trying to get rid of him.

"I am fine", Azim responded.

"Done with your skit preparation?" Kunal asked after a moment. "Almost!" Azim answered.

"You look tired, go drink some water. I am worried about you", Kunal again insisted. "No, I am good! No need to worry", Azim responded.

Kunal realized that he could not get rid of Azim. He strolled over to Sunaina and watched her exercise for some time.

"Wow! I can never do that... You have a flexible body", Kunal complimented.

Sunaina laughed at his compliment. Azim was still working on his skit but was eavesdropping on their conversation.

"Thank you, sir!" Sunaina thanked.

"Really! And please don't call me Sir. Just Kunal", he assured her. "Okay, Kunal."

"You have amazing talent and so much potential in you. I am sure you will make it big", Kunal flattered.

"I hope so. I am doing my best. Maybe, one day", Sunaina responded.

"You know what? I may be able to help you with that. I have a few contacts in B-Town. Also, at the end of this course you will meet many industry professionals", Kunal lured.

"Oh yeah? That's amazing", Sunaina acknowledged.

"But still, take my number. Call me if you need anything", Kunal offered. "Sure!" Sunaina replied. Anant entered the classroom with a plate of vada pav in his hands, searching for Sunaina. Anant walks towards Sunaina excitedly to offer her vada pav.

***

Here you go! Your *vada pav* and your green chili", Anant excitedly announced. "Seriously? That's too oily", Kunal commented.

"Yeah, I agree. I think I have to skip it. You have it, Anant", Sunaina kindly denied.

Anant insisted Sunaina on having the vada pav but she denies it.

Kunal left the classroom. Sunaina turned her head to watch him leave. Anant noticed this.

"Can I tell you something? Please don't take it personally", Anant checked. "Sure, go ahead", Sunaina replied.

"I don't think Kunal sir has good intentions", Anant manipulated. "What makes you say that?" Sunaina questioned.

"The way he looks at you. It feels kind of strange and weird", Anant justified. "Oh! So, you are jealous?" Sunaina quizzed.

"It's not like that. I just don't like it that he wants to talk to you alone", Anant replied.

"Anant, I do not like this clingy and controlling behavior. Please stop", Sunaina expunged. "Sorry, sorry! You got me all wrong", Anant corrected himself.

But Sunaina ignored him and left. Anant saddened by it dumps the vada pav in trash can.

***

Blackout on the stage, three silhouette of girls on centerstage appears to be present. Hiten enters the stage with Kunal behind him. "Welcome Sir, Welcome to my world-famous brothel Fuck Manch!" Hiten announced. He entered the room in a shiny shirt, with his hair combed and a spittoon in his hand. He was chewing tobacco paan.

Kunal followed him. "Thank you! What do you have for me today?" Kunal asked with an American accent. Kunal's costume was simple. He was wearing a floral shirt and he had sunglasses. He looked like he came from USA.

"I have wonderful booty-ful girls. You will love them", Hiten lured in the client.

Hiten escorted Kunal to the three girls - Jheel, Sunaina and Ragini, who were dressed in sexy costumes. Hiten pointed to Sunaina.

"The first is a beautiful flower from Kashmir, Kachhi Kali. She has cheeks as red as apples from Kashmir and a body that will make you salivate. You will be dying to get a taste. Baby, show us your talent", Hiten promoted.

Sunaina danced in a very erotic fashion for Kunal. "Wow! That's cool... Alright, alright!" Kunal complimented.

The next in line was Jheel.

"Sir, the next one is Virgin Rozy. A very tender flower. Watch her amazing, smooth, soft body. A beautiful piece of the moon she is", Hiten promoted, trying to touch Jheel's face.

She shoved his hand away.

"You will love her, I guarantee it!" Hiten added.

"Nice! Beautiful! But she is too young for me", Kunal ignored and moved on to next. Hiten finally pointed to Ragini.

"And lastly, we have Savita, the dark chocolate. She is the cheapest one we have. Only 200 rupees for an hour. This is for the economy class", Hiten promoted Ragini.

"Oh, I didn't even notice her in the dark. That's a big no!" Kunal said. "Yes, sir. Now please select one", Hiten requested.

Kunal looked at both women and then at Jheel. "You should be in school", he said. He looked at Sunaina and grabbed her hand before asking Hiten. "How much for her?" Kunal asked.

"500 rup… dollars!" Hiten replied. "Okay! Done!" Kunal exclaimed.

Kunal exited the stage with Sunaina while Hiten took a bow. Even though it was a skit, the others were feeling bad for Ragini. Hiten's behavior towards her was offensive. Anant felt insecure and angry after seeing Kunal and Sunaina together.

"Are you done, Hiten?" Kanika questioned. She asked Kunal and Sunaina to come in. They entered holding hands but quickly let go.

"This is your reality, isn't it? Are you a pimp or are you a client?" Kanika asked. "Actually, you don't have to answer that!"

"I'm a pimp!" Hiten said boastingly.

"I expected that", Kanika replied.

"I am always impressed by how well you understand me", Hiten acknowledged.

"Well, I am your teacher. Now, feedback time. Everyone did a great job and I especially like that everyone had a unique character", Kanika gave her feedback. After her feedback, Kanika noticed that Ragini was hurt. "Ragini, are you okay?" Kanika asked.

Ragini was reminiscing about her past incidents .

"Ragini? Ragini?" Kanika checked on her. "Yeah", Ragini replied.

"Remember, whatever happens in the imaginary world stays in the imaginary world", Kanika reminded her.

Ragini nodded in agreement and left to take her seat when Kanika stopped her. "Let's do yours now, Ragini", she insisted.

"Okay", Ragini replied.

***

The cast for Ragini's skit included Kanika, Azim, and Jheel. Ragini told the actors where to stand and set up the scene. Kunal gestured to Ragini to begin the play.

"Ding-Dong! Ding-Dong!" Kunal mimicked the sound of a doorbell. The sound took Ragini to an incident that happened in the past. The skit was based on this very incident.

***

In the real-life version, Ragini's family was awaiting guests, a couple who were supposed to visit them that day. Anita, Kamal and Mohini welcomed the guests as they entered the house. Ragini was forced to go to her room and stay there during their visit.

"*Namastey! Namastey*! Brother! How are you?" Anita welcomed them with a smile. "*Namastey! Namastey*! All good?" Rimi asked.

"Were there any issues getting here?" Kamal asked. "No, No. No issues at all", Rahul clarified.

"Good! Mohini, please get those…" Kamal was about to ask Mohini to bring the snacks when she walked in with the tray.

"Wow! She is very beautiful", Rimi complimented and helped herself to a samosa from the tray.

"Yes, I think she took after me", Anita said. After dinner, Rimi wanted to use the restroom. "Where is the restroom?" Rimi asked.

"Just go straight and it will be the second door on the right", Anita guided.

Rimi excused herself and walked towards the restroom. When she got to the door, she tried to open it but the door would not open. She pressed hard to open the door. Ragini unlocked the door and stepped out. Seeing Ragini, a startled Rimi yelled in fear. Anita ran towards the restroom.

"Who is this?" Rimi asked, pointing to Ragini.

Anita turned to Ragini and yelled, "How many times have I told you not to use this restroom? There is society restroom outside for you. Now, go inside and don't come out. You are scaring our guests."

"Oh my god! I couldn't even see her in the dark!" Rimi commented. "Like father, like daughter", Anita muttered to herself, but Rimi heard it. "What?" Rimi asked.

"Nothing, leave it." Anita diverted. "By the way your saree is stunning. Where did you get it?" She changed the topic.

"From the market", Rimi replied. Once Rimi used the restroom, the ladies went back and joined the rest of the family in the living room.

"What happened?" Kamal asked.

"Nothing. Our maid scared her", Anita explained. "Leave it. It's okay", Rimi replied.

"It's getting late, we should leave", Rahul said after a while. He turned to the couple and said, "Thank you so much for inviting us for dinner."

"Thank you. It was nice meeting you", Rimi commented. "It was our pleasure. Do visit us again", Kamal greeted. "*Namastey*!" Anita said, bidding them goodbye.

The moment the guests were gone Anita looked at Kamal angrily.

***

The actors in the studio enacting the scene did the same. Kanika looking angrily at Azim.

"I told her not to come out. This dumbass girl never listens. Now I must teach her a lesson", Kanika cursed.

"RAGINI! RAGINI!" Kanika shouted. Ragini entered the stage, shaking with fear.

"How many times did I tell you to stay in your room? How many times did I tell you not to come out when guests are around? You did it on purpose, didn't you?" Kanika yelled.

"Sorry mother, I really needed to use the restroom", Ragini replied.

"How dare you talk back to me?" Kanika said, angrily. "Wait, I'm going to show you..." she trailed off.

***

In the real-life version, Anita went into the kitchen and brought a hot pair of tongs. She wanted to burn her own daughter's hands and face as a punishment.

Seeing this, Ragini tried calling out for her father. "Have you gone mad?" Kamal stopped her.

"Yes, I have gone mad. Now you stay silent. It is all your fault", Anita blamed Kamal.

Anita took the hot pair of tongs and burnt Ragini's hand with it before

Kamal could reach out to save her. Ragini screamed in pain.

"Are you going to kill her? She is our daughter", Kamal questioned.

"She is not my daughter. My daughter could never look like this. Look at me! Look how fair I am. I feel ashamed to call her my daughter", Anita said while Ragini cried in pain.

***

Ragini was tending to her burnt hand with Azim and Jheel by her side while Kanika shouted at her.

"I feel ashamed that you are my daughter. Go to your room", Kanika chastised.

Ragini sat there crying and taking in what Kanika had said. Then suddenly, she exploded.

"I feel ashamed to call you my mother! Mother? Do you even know what mother means? A mother is supposed to protect her child. She does not harm or burn them", Ragini screamed in pain, but this time, it was emotional. "You call yourself a mother? You have not done anything that a mother should! People consider themselves lucky to have a mother, but I feel doomed to have a mother like you! It would've been better if I was an orphan. Did you ever love me? I've been longing for your love! But all you ever did was put me down and despise me." Ragini burst into tears as Kanika looked at her furiously. "You know what? Go to hell! Go to hell all of you! I don't give a damn."

"Yes, this is the ugly truth. Society is obsessed with fair skin. Every motherfucker wants to be fair skinned. Since we were children, we were taught that being fair means you are beautiful and being dark means you are ugly! Even in our schoolbooks, there were pictures teaching us the same thing. This is what children learn today.

Dark children in schools are bullied. They are given funny names. Our education, media and society are all at fault for this.

Become fair in just two weeks! This is what fairness creams tell us. Bloody fuckers are fooling people to make money. And not to forget actors who are brand ambassadors for these products. They should feel ashamed to endorse these things. Shame on you and shame on the people who have this sick mentality!"

Ragini stopped her outburst to take a deep breath and control her voice.

"I say FUCK YOU! and FUCK FAIR SKIN! FUCK SOCIETY! I do not want to become fair. Yes, I am dark, So fucking what? I'm fucking happy with my skin tone. I'm happy that I am dark and I am proud of it", Ragini concluded.

Everyone in the class was taken aback by Ragini's monologue. The entire class immediately stood up and applauded for her. Hiten too, cheered for her.

"Great job, Ragini." Everyone admired her outburst. Ragini smiled at them weakly with tears in her eyes.

Chapter 7

Jheel is waiting impatiently for her friend Zui in the park. After a while, Zui walks in anger towards Jheel. She takes out her bag and hands a bag full of clothes and accessories to Jheel.

"Here! This is all yours.", Zui exclaimed in angst. Jheel starts going through the stuff, takes out a paper from her pocket and marks a tick on the paper. Zui reacts to this ridiculousness. "I didn't expect you to be this cheap!!", Zui mocked Jheel. Zui turns and starts walking. Jheel realizes that something is missing. "Hey wait", Jheel stopped Zui. "My Hoop earrings are missing!!", Jheel notified Zui. "You gifted me the hoop earrings!", Zui reminded Jheel. "I lent you the earrings. You never returned.", Jheel accused Zui. "You never asked... They were with me for three years.", Zui retorted. "Now they won't be!", Jheel demanded Zui of her earrings.

"Fine! I will find it and give it back!!", Zui handed over the earring to Jheel. Zui notices the green jacket which she gave to Jheel long back. "And what about this Green Jacket you are wearing?", Zui interrogated Jheel. Jheel takes the green jacket and gives it to her. "There you go!", Jheel handed the jacket to Zui. "Thanks. And just to be clear. I don't want you to tell anyone that you slapped Aayush.", Zui ordered Jheel. "Fine. I don't even want to think about him. He is an asshole!", Jheel retorted. "Hey! He is my boyfriend!! Okay!", Zui warned Jheel. "Yeah! And surprisingly you don't get it! He is a pervert!!", Jheel attacked Zui. "At least he is not like your Dad!!!", Zui offended Jheel with her retort. Right after, Zui realizes that she shouldn't have said it. Jheel is shocked to hear that and is hurt, her eyes are watery. Zui goes closer to Jheel and holds her. "Please you can't tell anybody what I told you about my parents.", Jheel pleaded Zui. "I am really sorry! I shouldn't have said that.", Zui apologized Jheel. "Promise me! you won't tell anything about my parents. Right?", Jheel requested Zui. Zui comforts and hugs Jheel while she is crying.

"I promise I won't. You know what you were right! I am gonna leave Aayush! He is an Asshole!", Zui promised Jheel and tried to make her feel good.

***

Meanwhile in the studio, Ragini and Azim were the first to be in the studio the next day. They were discussing their notes and talking about acting techniques. Hiten walked into the class and strode right up to Azim and Ragini as if he was about to pick a fight with them. Following Hiten, Jheel, Sunaina and Anant too entered the studio and saw Hiten with a box. Everyone gathered around to see what was about to happen. But Hiten produced a box of cupcakes with a flourish.

"*Namastey*! This is for you", Hiten said while he handed them the cupcakes. "I'm really sorry. I behaved very discourteously with the two of you. Please forgive me, it will not happen again." He was the embodiment of politeness.

Both Ragini and Azim were taken aback by this sudden change in Hiten's behavior. They did not know what to say or do.

"This is a new start of our friendship", Hiten said, proposing a toast with the cupcake.

Azim and Ragini were surprised and hesitant about taking a cupcake. Ragini went ahead and took one, but she held it in her hand without eating it. "You didn't mix anything in this? Did you?" Ragini asked.

Nothing I will eat and show you", Hiten responded. He picked up a cupcake and gobbled it down quickly. "Now can you trust me?" Hiten asked.

Ragini and Azim glanced at each other before taking a bite of their cupcakes. "Everyone gathered around", Hiten invited them to take a cupcake.

Jheel and Sunaina were the first to come up and grab a cupcake, but Anant was still hesitant. This kind gesture by Hiten gave Azim some hope that he would be able to get some closure on the kiss they shared.

***

Meanwhile Kanika and Kunal were having a fight in the cabin of Kalamanch. "This is not done", Kunal warned.

"But she needs to know the truth", Kanika responded.

"What is the need for that? I told you that this should never come out. That was our deal!" Kunal reminded.

"Kunal, we also had a deal about always being honest with each other. I cannot hide this from my child", Kanika retorted.

"She is my child, you are her stepmother. You are pushing me away from her. Don't you see that?" Kunal warned her.

"I'm not doing anything", Kanika denied.

"She is not talking to me now from past three days and it's all your fault. Is this what you want?" Kunal asked.

"Are you mad? If this is all I wanted, then I would've done it a long time ago. Give her some time", Kanika explained.

"You know what? Do not try to take her away from me", Kunal warned.

"I'm the one taking her away from you? You should know what a great father you are. When she needed you, you were busy fucking someone else", Kanika exploded.

"You are a fucking bitch!" Kunal shouted and slapped her across the face. He stormed out of the office and slammed the door on his way out leaving Kanika in stunned disbelief.

***

Back in the classroom, everyone was savoring the cupcakes Hiten had brought. Azim walked to Hiten to have a word with him.

"The cupcakes were nice… It was a nice gesture", Azim complimented. "Yeah, thanks", Hiten replied.

"Ragini looks happy…" Azim remarked. "Yes!"

Awkward silence filled the air between them.

"Are you ready for the skit? You remember everything, right?" Azim asked. "Yes. But I am going to leave early today; I have to go to the temple." Azim was confused on Hiten's behavior, "And one more thing… what happened… that day…" Azim reminded.

"Which day?" Hiten asked. Faking a call on his phone, he deflected, "Wait, man. I'm getting a call… I'll talk to you later." Hiten ran out to take the fake call.

Azim looked at him confused and Ragini was approached him.

"Hey, what happened?" Ragini checked. "Nothing… I… I just need a partner for the skit."

"I'm there for you. I am ready to be your partner any time", Ragini tried to cheer him up.

"Yeah, I know… But I needed a guy." Azim explained.

"I can be your guy! I can be anything you want…" Ragini offered her help.

"Thanks", Azim surprised at her.

Ragini hugged him tight, and Azim realized that something was different with Ragini.

"Okay guys! Everyone is here… Let's get started", Kanika addressed the class. "Wait!" Sunaina stopped. "Kunal is not here…"

Its time We will start without him", Kanika instructed and began the exercise.

"Okay ma'am", Anant said. He then noticed Kanika's cheek and asked her, "Ma'am, what happened to your cheek? It's very red." Anant inquired.

"It's just a rash. Thanks for asking Anyway, we will now start with

Jheel's act", Kanika pretends to be fine and hides her cheek.

"Ma'am, you and Kunal sir are in my skit; I can't find Kunal sir." Jheel mentioned. "He must be outside; he will come", Kanika reasoned.

"Let me check…" Sunaina insisted. "I am going out and I will send him in." Kanika and Anant noticed her assertiveness and were uncomfortable.

***

Sunaina walked out of the building and went into the parking lot looking for Kunal. She noticed him smoking in the parking lot near his car and approached him.

"Hey!" Sunaina greeted "Hey!" Kunal replied in really low voice

Sunaina asked "What happened?" "Nothing much, just the usual", Kunal replied.

"Okay, no problem. By the way, Jheel is looking for you", Sunaina said and walked towards the building when Kunal stopped her.

"Would you like one?" Kunal asked, offering her a cigarette.

"Sure… I really need it", Sunaina exclaimed, taking the cigarette from his hand. He lit it for her. "When did you start smoking?" Kunal asked.

"Long time ago… Don't even remember… Probably in my teens." Sunaina answered. "Is Anant okay with this?" Kunal asked.

"He asks me not to smoke, but I don't care. I don't like being controlled", Sunaina answered. "Are you and Anant serious?" Kunal asked.

"No… Nothing serious. I mean… we were for a little while, but now I'm confused", Sunaina tried to explain.

"Why?" Kunal asked. "Because he is divorced or because he is older than you?"

"No... I don't care about divorce, or his age, but I don't like clingy guys. I like dating many people; I'm not a monogamist. You know what I mean? Now, things have become so weird..." Sunaina tried to gather her thoughts. After a few moments, she said, "Never mind."

"Yeah, I can understand", Kunal said.

"By the way, you and Kanika are a very cool couple. I loved hearing all your stories", Sunaina complimented, trying to change the topic.

"Cool couple!" Kunal laughed sarcastically. "Yeah, right!" "Why, what happened?" Sunaina asked.

"Kanika, umm..." Kunal shook his head. "It's all her fault. These days she does whatever she wants." Kunal complained.

Sunaina nodded.

"A few days back, she, I mean Kanika... told something to my... our... daughter, Kashish. I wish she had not said it. Certain things are not supposed to be said to kids..." Kunal lowered his voice, She told her "I cheated on her real mom Khushi." Kunal opened up to Sunaina.

"You did?" Sunaina asked.

Kunal ignored her question. "And now Kashish refuses to talk to me..."

"Oh, Kunal... I'm sorry. I hope everything turns out okay", Sunaina tried to comfort him.

There was a moment of silence. Kunal said, "You know, I envy you. I want to live like you — open, free! Marriage is an unconscious bondage. You cannot live alone so you become dependent on the other; the other cannot live alone so he or she becomes dependent on you. And we hate the person on whom we are dependent; nobody likes to depend on anybody."

"Yeah, that is true…" Sunaina agreed.

"Our deepest desire is to have freedom, total freedom. And dependence… is against freedom."

Sunaina and Kunal knew they were attracted to each other. Jheel interrupted them saying, "Kunal sir, I need you."

"Yeah, coming…" Kunal said. "Let's go!" Sunaina said.

***

As Kanika, and Kunal were preparing for the skit with Jheel. Jheel stepped forward and tapped Kunal on the shoulder.

"You are my dad, Neel. You are Neel", Jheel reminded.

"Okay… Wait, how does your dad hold the newspaper?", Kunal asked, taking the newspaper into his hands, "…like this?"

"Yes", Jheel said.

"Why don't we start?" Kanika insisted. "And Jheel, you can stop us at any time."

Jheel nodded and stepped back, taking her position. There was silence in the room. "Kunal", Kanika started.

Kunal continued reading his newspaper.

"Kunal, I mean Neel. Neel, I need to speak to you." "I'm busy", Kunal ignored.

"You are reading the newspaper." Kanika sarcastically called out, "This newspaper is important to me." Kunal ignored. "Pay attention to me, Neel.", Kanika said

Kunal lowers the newspaper after a second. "What is it?" Kunal said frustratingly. "I am lonely", Kanika said.

"So? I am lonely, too. All of us are lonely. Extremely alone." Kunal enlightened.

"Then why do you ignore me? Why do you always read or watch TV? When you actually should talk to Jheel… talk to me!" Kanika complained.

Kunal ignored Kanika. "Why don't you talk to me?" Kanika questioned him.

"You are very neurotic", Kunal said, angrily.

Jheel piped in. "He wouldn't say that. I mean, my dad wouldn't think that way." "What would he think?" Kanika asked Jheel.

"He would say that she was always nagging him", Jheel instructed. "You are always nagging me", Kunal starts again. "Maybe that is because you keep ignoring me.", Kanika said with pain.

"Maybe I ignore you because you're driving me crazy." Kunal said with irritation.

"Then leave me, Neel. Why don't you just leave us and go?" Kanika grilled him. "Because I am stuck…", Kunal said, impulsively.

"Yes, I am stuck too," Kanika exclaims. Because of you… I left my career behind, sat at home, took care of you and Jheel…and that's how you treat me?" Kanika said.

"Did I ask you… to leave it behind?", Kunal asked.

"Please don't fight", Jheel pleaded. She was in tears. But they were too deep into their daily squabbles to pay attention to her.

"Ask me as in? Now you don't value my sacrifices at all. I did everything for you… despite what you have done to me… because I love you, and you… you are a selfish person! You don't even care for Jheel", Kanika yelled.

"I…" Kunal paused and winced, as if he was in pain.

"Just because you're angry with me, that doesn't mean you shouldn't talk to Jheel, or behave with her this way", Kanika complained.

"She will never forgive me", Kunal said. As tears started rolling from his eyes. "She loves you, Neel", Kanika explained.

Kunal rubbed his eyes, he was crying. "I…um…" Kunal tried to speak.

"What?" Kanika inquired. "I am ashamed." Kunal admitted.

"Of what? For what?" Kanika asked.

"For my…" Kunal paused. "About my life… I want something else."

"But Jheel isn't judging you, Neel." Kanika paused. "She just needs her dad." Kanika then placed her fingers on Kunal's chin and lifted it. "Neel, look at me."

Kunal looked at her with tears in his eyes.

"Jheel just needs your love. She needs your attention. That's all you have to do", she explained.

Kunal nodded and looked at Kanika and Jheel sadly. Kanika broke down and looked at Jheel who was crying. Kanika hugged her.

"It's okay Jheel, let it out", Kanika consoled her. "Guys, we'll take a small break", she told the class.

Jheel stayed behind in class while the others left the room. The skit has been so close to what happened in her childhood every single day, except that Kunal had not flung beer bottles to the floor like her father, Neel, and he had not called Kanika a fucking whore like her father had called her mother.

***

When everyone came back from the break, Kanika continued with the class. "Jheel, you okay now?" Kanika asked.

"Yes, ma'am", Jheel replied.

"Good!" Kanika placed her hand on Jheel's hair.

She turned to the class. "Good job, everyone! See guys, the thing about Jheel's skit was that she had minimal dialogues. The main thing was that she was listening and reacting to everything that was happening. So, listening is very important. It's not just the dialogue you need to listen to. There are also underlying actions that are important to take note of. To demonstrate this, we will play a small game. I need two volunteers — one guy and one girl", Kanika said.

Sunaina and Ragini stood up, but Sunaina won the spot.

When Sunaina won, Anant and Kunal also stood up.

Kunal won by pushing Anant on side.

"Alright, Sunaina and Kunal, stand here facing each other. You will have to say a few things to each other but in your own gibberish language.

After you are done, we will guess and discuss what you said to each other. Okay?" Kanika explained.

The class nodded.

Kanika gave the exercise a go.

"*Uu… Jo…*" Kunal uttered in his gibberish. In his mind, he meant *hello*.

"*Haa lish*!" Sunaina replied figuring out her own gibberish, which was her way of saying *hello*. "*Uu Jo?*" Kunal said again.

"*Haalish Haalish!*" Sunaina replied again. "*Uu Jo*" Kunal excitedly said again to get the game going.

"*Haalish… Haalish Haalish Haalish…*" Sunaina said. She meant *I have something to*

tell you. "*Uu Jo?*" Kunal asked. He meant *what is it?*

"*Haalish Haalish Haalish Haalish Haalish…*" Sunaina replied. Her way of saying

Sometimes at night I feel incredibly lonely.

"*Uu Jo Uu Jo?*" Kunal said, which meant *I don't understand what you are saying.*

"*Haalish Haalish Haalish Haalish, Haalish Haalish Haalish Haalish,*

Haalish Haalish Haalish Haalish", Sunaina replied, which meant *I lie in bed staring at the ceiling and I think about couples and families like you and Kanika.*

"Uu Jo Uu Jo Uu Jo Uu Jo…" Kunal said, *you are very beautiful.* *"Haalish Halish Haalish?"* Sunaina said, *are you sad too?*

"Uu Jo", Kunal said, ``*I am attracted to you.*

"Haalish Haalish Haalish Haalish…" Sunaina said, *you are sad too. I knew it.*

"Uu Jo Uu Jo Uu Jo Uu Jo…" Kunal said, *I feel really guilty when I think about how attracted I am to you.*

"Haalish Haalish", Sunaina said after a long pause. *I feel like you understand me.* *"Uu Jo Uu Jo"*, Kunal said. *I feel like you actually understand me.*

They gazed at each other. They felt a deep connection. The connection was such that even the students felt it and Kanika was uncomfortable. She blurted out.

"Okay. Good! Stop. What do you think? What were they talking about?" Kanika addressed the students.

"They seemed to be lost in each other. There was a deep feeling growing between the two", Azim said.

"I did not like it at all!", Anant expressed disagreement.

"They were in love", Jheel exclaimed. There was a long, uncomfortable silence.

"Okay, that just happened in the imaginary world, but what do you think they were talking about?" Kanika asked.

"At first she was upset", Ragini commented.

"It felt like she was trying to share some secret", Azim analyzed. "Kind of like a proposal", Jheel added.

"It almost felt like Kunal sir could understand Sunaina", Azim stated what he felt.

While everyone discussed what Kunal and Sunaina had tried to say to each other, the duo exchanged romantic glances. While Anant and Kanika observed their behavior, both their faces turned pale with worry. "We will take a small break before wrapping up things for today", Kanika dismissed the class and rushed to her cabin.

***

During the break Anant was sulking in the hallway. He was shattered and his self-confidence was destroyed after what he had just witnessed. He picked up his bag and rushed to Kanika's cabin with tears in his eyes.

"Ma'am, I need to talk to you", Anant shivered into her office in distraught. "Sure, come in. Take a seat. Everything alright?" Kanika inquired.

Kanika saw the look on his face. She saw that something was bothering him. "Are you okay?" Kanika checked on Anant, worried.

"Ma'am, I will not be able to continue anymore. I'm leaving. If I ever did anything wrong to hurt anyone, please forgive me", Anant pleaded.

"Leaving? What do you mean?" Kanika enquired.

"Ma'am I respect you with all my heart, but how do I say this? I just... I don't have it in me", Anant cried.

"Have what? What are you talking about?" Kanika asked, confused.

"Ma'am, I cannot be an actor, I do not have it in me. I don't have any personality, confidence, nor do I know how to speak English properly. Everyone laughs at me. Everyone thinks I'm a joke. I can't even perform in front of the class because I know it will lead to insults", Anant expressed his inner turmoil. He felt so down and underestimated himself. He felt a sense of loss which took him back to a place where he was underconfident like in the beginning of the acting program.

"One minute, who told you all this? Everything that you are saying is in your past. I've seen you grow a lot since the day one. You do have everything inside you that can make you a good actor", Kanika motivated Anant.

"Ma'am, please forgive me", Anant apologized. He joined his palms together and bowed his head. Kanika didn't accept his apology and took Anant by the hand and led him to the classroom. Everyone was present there except Kunal and Sunaina who left early.

"Everyone, stop what you are doing and listen to me! This guy here wants to leave the class. He wants to quit acting and says that he cannot become an actor. He does not have it in him. How many of you agree with that?" Kanika questioned her students.

No one raised their hands.

"See Anant? No one thinks like that.", Kanika enlightened Anant.

"Anyone can be an actor. It does not matter where you come from, whether you are an introvert or extrovert, what the color of your skin is, whether you are tall, short, thin, or fat. Whether you know English or not. You can be physically disabled, but it does not matter as long as you are passionate about the craft.", Kanika electrified the students. "You need to have that thirst inside you to learn and grow. If you have that determination to learn, no one can ever push you back. So, I will not allow you or anyone else here to quit. We are all in this together", Kanika inspired the students.

Anant was deeply moved by the speech of Kanika as he replied with a deep sense of conviction which was never seen during the past six weeks" I will become an actor" Anant declared in confidence. Everyone in the class joined Anant and repeated "Yes we will become an actor" and gave Anant a group hug. Kanika was so proud of all her students as she smiled. It was a victory for her as an acting teacher that her students are supportive of each other and are very open now.

The End.

Epilog

That night, Anant came out of his bathroom with a smile on his face. He was going to call Sunaina. He went to his bed, sat down, and picked up his phone to make a call.

***

In a parked car, two shadows were kissing and moaning in pleasure. Their phones were on the dashboard, vibrating due to incoming calls. Kunal's phone screen flashed 'Kanika'. Sunaina's phone showed 'Anant'.

***

Hiten was on his terrace confused about his sexual orientation.

***

In Azim's bedroom, Ragini and Azim were naked and spooning each other.

***

Jheel was on her bed with her laptop. She typed in Anant's name, and his profile showed up.

Recommendation for playwrights

1. William Shakespeare
2. Moliere
3. Bernard Shaw
4. Henrik Ibsen
5. Oscar Wilde
6. Anton Chekhov
7. Neil Simon
8. Neil LaBute
9. Arthur Miller
10. Eugene O'Neil
11. Tennessee Williams
12. Samuel Beckett
13. Harold Pinter
14. Noel Coward
15. August Wilson
16. T.S. Eliot
17. John Osborne

18.   Annie Baker

19.   David Mamet

20.   Sam Shepard

21.   Ayad Akhtar

22.   Rajiv Joseph

Recommendation for Performance art's books -

1. Audition by Michael Shurtleff

2. Respect for acting by Uta Hagen

3. The intent to live by Larry Moss

4. Freeing the natural voice by Kristin Linklater

5. Acting as a business by Brian O'Neil

6. The actor's art and craft by Damon DiMarco, William Esper

7. Shakespeare, Shamans, and Show Biz by David Kaplan

8. The Unlimited Actor by Nancy Mayans

9. Classically speaking by Patricia Fletcher

10. Body Learning: An Introduction to the Alexander Technique by Michael J. Gelb

11. Sanford Meisner on Acting

12. Actions: The Actors' Thesaurus by Marina Caldarone

13. The art of Acting by Stella Adler

14. Learning your lines, the compact guide by Mark Channon.

15. Improvisation for the Theatre by Viola Spolin

16. Loving to Audition by Larry Silverberg

17. Zen and the art of archery by Eugene Herrigel

18. The Artists Way by Julia Cameron

www.ingramcontent.com/pod-product-compliance
Lightning Source LLC
LaVergne TN
LVHW091611170726
843492LV00007B/2354